Diamond White

A Red Riley Adventure #2

Stephanie Andrews

Diamond White

A Red Riley Adventure #2

Copyright 2017 by Stephanie Andrews.

Published by Piscataqua Press

32 Daniel St. Portsmouth, NH 03801

Printed in the United States

www.andewsauthor.com

join the newsletter, get good karma
and a free novella

The Red Riley Adventures

Chicago Blue
Diamond White
Solid Gold
Agent Orange
Deep Sea Green

The Levelers

The Grafton Heist
The Train Job

I was at Ruby's place on Nippersink Lake on a frigid December day when Selena Salerno caught up with me. It was a moment I had dreaded for months, hoping it would never happen. Now it had.

When the silent alarm went off, I hoped it was a mistake. A deer, or maybe just the wind blowing so hard it tripped a sensor. The wind chill made it feel like Antarctica outside, and I wasn't that excited about suiting up to trudge the quarter mile to the perimeter. But Marty had assured me that this security system was excellent, and after a few calibrations of the cameras in the beginning, they seemed to be doing their job.

I picked up a walkie-talkie off the kitchen counter.

"El, come in. El, are you reading me?"

There was a long pause, and then a labored voice answered.

"I read you, Kay. How much of this damn wood do I have to chop?"

"How warm do you want to be?"

"I'm actually sweating right now. And my arms are killing me."

"Can you check on camera six? The alarm went off."

"Will do. Can I come in after that?"

"I'm sorry," I said, repeatedly thumbing the button. "You're breaking up."

I turned off the talkie and stepped to the computer desk on the glassed-in porch. I'm pretty sure that before Ruby bought the house the old fisherman who owned it used this area as a fly-tying workbench. There was a battered countertop with a tiny little vice mounted on it, and old pegboard attached to the wall above. The house, for the most part, did not smell like old fish. For the most part. There was still some painting and renovation to do.

Diamond White

It had only been six months since I became a ghost. Someday I'll sell the book and movie rights, and you'll be able to get the whole story. Short version: I was an unassuming Chicago police officer, who was wrongly thought to have been a criminal mastermind determined to bring down two large telecom firms. When the dust settled, I was exonerated, but believed to have been killed in a huge explosion at my apartment.

Only a handful of people knew that I'd survived, and only Ruby and her nephew Marty knew that I had managed to walk off with a few million dollars, which I shared with them. Ruby bought this secluded cabin in the woods, where I spend most of my time training, and Marty leased a large office in downtown Chicago to expand his business, Technology Acquired.

The alarm went off again, making me jump. Silent alarms are only silent at the point of contact. This one was loud in the quiet of the control room. Okay, the back porch. I was still working on all the nomenclature, but "control room" sounded pretty awesome.

I scanned the feed of the six cameras, but all I could see was white. It had snowed hard the previous night and was still snowing lightly. I peered closely at the picture, which was sharp, but small and in black and white. It's possible that I needed reading glasses.

There! Something was moving through the trees, all but invisible in this weather. There it was again. A person, dressed all in white, was moving effortlessly in the deep snow, flitting like a ghost. I leaned closer and closer, until my face was inches from the monitor. The intruder leapt nimbly over a fallen log. They wore a skintight white body suit that covered them from head to toe, with only a small cutout for the face, which was mostly obscured by a pair of tinted goggles, and another cut out for the pony tail.

2

Diamond White

I leapt back from the screen and gasped. Crap. It could only be one person. The agility, the audacity, and the fashion sense all told me it had to be Salerno. What on Earth had I done to deserve this?

I raced back to the kitchen and grabbed wildly at the walkie-talkie, knocking over and smashing a drinking glass in the process. I frantically pushed the talk button, repeatedly, then realized the power was off.

Hitting the switch, I hissed, "El! El! Park, do you copy? Stand down. Stand down now!" I was going to be the first spy in history to get their sidekick killed in the very first scene. I knew I should've have stayed solo. There was no response from the radio. I tried again. "Stand down," I whispered. "In fact, hide. Hide and call Ruby," I added, realizing that the noise from the talkie could attract Salerno's attention.

Thank God I already had my boots on, because those suckers took forever to lace up. I threw on my quilted jacket and ran outside and down the back steps. There was a utility shed between the house and the woods, and I slogged my way to it through the snow. Hanging on the back of the shed were two bright blue kayaks, and I pulled a paddle from one of them. It was rudimentary as far as weapons go, but at least it would be something. Damn, my fingers were already freezing, but my gloves were inside and it was too late to go back; I could hear the soft crunching of someone making their way cautiously through the snow.

I centered myself and controlled my breathing. By holding one hand lightly over my nose and mouth and exhaling slowly, I made sure that my visible breath didn't extend beyond the corner of the shed.

I waited. And waited. The steps sounded closer, yet they barely made a sound. For a moment, I panicked. What if it were El sneaking back to the cabin? No, the

Diamond White

movement was too quiet, almost indiscernible. In fact, I was just beginning to wonder if I was actually hearing it at all when suddenly, a cloud of vapor drifted past the end of the shed.

I stepped forward, shouting a kiyup , and swung the paddle with both hands. Sure enough, the intruder was right there. She managed to get her forearm up to block the blow, but the force of it sent her into the side of the shed with a thud. Still, she was able to kick her leg out, strong and high, and catch me in the hip as I turned through my swing. The force knocked me sideways onto the ground. The snow was packed here in the middle of the yard, and I purposefully rolled away from her, eight or ten feet, still clutching he paddle, before I jumped back up to a ready position.

She laughed that deep-throated, sultry laugh of hers, pulling off her goggles and smiling at me. It was her alright. She reached up and pulled off the hood, shaking her head and flipping her long brown ponytail from side to side. I took the opportunity to step forward and take a swing at her head, but she saw me coming and side-stepped the paddle.

"Red," she said, still with a smile on her face. "I'm not here to fight you, honestly." She held out her hands, palm up, as if in supplication. I took a step toward her, and with a lightning-fast move she grabbed the end of the paddle and yanked. I was holding it in my left hand, which was missing the ring and pinky fingers, so my grip was poor and she easily snatched the paddle away. I kicked myself for making a rookie mistake, pushing my hair out of my eyes and backing up slowly as she advanced. A few steps more and I passed the large woodchopping block, continuing to backpedal until my lower back hit the neatly stacked woodpile. I looked for the axe but it was nowhere around.

4

Diamond White

"You've got to be freezing in that outfit," I told her. Delay and diversion were two of my strongest assets, and among the only ones currently at my disposal. "How did you find me?"

"Well, after our incident with the diamonds, it was clear you weren't dead." She began to circle slowly around the chopping stump, and I matched her step-for-step in a slow clockwise circle. "Nice, job, by the way. Pulling that off."

We had circled one and a half times around the stump, both wary.

"Anyway," she continued, "it took some digging to find that your friend has a secluded cottage in the countryside. I thought it was worth a look. *Eschúcha*, I'm only here because I need your help."

That seemed unlikely. It was true that I had helped her, probably even saved her life, but I didn't think she knew about that, what I had done, or even that it was me. Besides, what could she possibly need my help for? She was a one-woman strike force.

"Well, that is interesting—"

I was interrupted by Ellery Park, who had been hiding behind the wood pile the whole time. She popped into view behind Selena, holding the axe backward, gripping the handle just below the blade. Before I could say or do anything she struck Salerno hard across the back of the head with the butt of the axe.

Selena dropped to the ground, groaning. Deep red blood flowed from her head into the white snow as El and I rushed to her side. I scooped up a handful of snow and held it against the back of her head where the gash was. She tried to roll over, but I lightly put my knee on her back, just to keep her in place.

"Woah," said El, somewhat in shock. "Do you think she really wanted your help?"

Diamond White

"I don't know," I said. "Good thing you didn't use the sharp end, or we'd never find out. Let's get her inside."

So, the Diamond Affair, as I like to call it. What follows is the whole story. Get yourself a tall drink and some snacks, because it's another riveting tale of how I almost got myself killed, and how through luck, good friends, and a little quick thinking, I survived.

Plus, you're probably wondering where the Ellery Park woman came from. Hey, every great vigilante needs a sidekick. I'll explain her presence as well.

Here's where the swirly flashback music would normally play.

It all started in September, about three months after the whole nightmare with Illcom and Farnham, the telecom giants, which had ended with me presumed dead.

I was sitting at a table at the Palm Court in Arlington Heights, a good way outside Chicago, just to be safe. Across from me, using a piece of bread to sop up the last of the gravy from his plate, was Nick Shelby.

Nick had promised me a date if I cleared my name and was still alive at the end of it. Well, I did and I was, and now he was keeping up his end of the bargain.

It was a fantastic dinner, and the company was pretty good, too. Nick is tall, with dark wavy hair and dark brown puppy-dog eyes behind dork glasses. He seems to have a permanent three-day beard, which is hilarious, because it comes from forgetting to shave. It certainly isn't a fashion statement, because Nick has no sense of fashion. Although that night he seemed to have made an effort. He was wearing a black suit with faint grey pinstripes, and a sparkling white shirt with no tie.

I was wearing a stunning emerald green sleeveless dress that showed off the new muscles in my shoulders and triceps. My hair was its natural red, styled into a pixie cut. I was probably going to grow it long again— I hadn't

Diamond White

enjoyed having a shaved head— but in the meantime, I was playing up the whole Audrey Hepburn vibe, and it seemed to be working on Nick. He likes to act aloof, but I repeatedly caught him staring at me when he thought I wasn't looking.

I pushed my plate away. I had stuck to a salad and French onion soup, not because I didn't like steak, but because I was still super self-conscious about my hand. Not only did it look incredibly creepy and unsettling, with its strange, scarred pink skin where the fingers should be, but it was hard to use a knife and fork at the same time. I was learning, but it was taking a while. I mostly kept my left hand under the table, on my lap, while I ate.

As we left the restaurant, Nick stopped me in the lobby, turning me around and pushing me back against the beige wall. I raised my eyebrows and grinned.

"Here, sir? I thought we might wait until we got to your place."

He stepped back and reached into his inside jacket pocket. In one quick motion, he removed his iPhone, snapped a picture of me, and returned it to his pocket.

"Hey!" I cried. "What was that for?"

"I just want to remember our first date," he said, and took my good hand to lead me out to his car.

"Well," I said, in my sultriest voice, "the best way to do that is to make it memorable."

"Oh," said Nick. "What did you have in mind?"

"The better question is what don't I have in mind..."

Later, we were in bed. He was on his back and I was straddling him. I put my arms above my head and stretched luxuriously, then looked down at him with a grin.

"That," I said, "was excellent."

"I agree," he murmured, running a hand along my side and over my hip. "Your body is getting amazing."

Diamond White

"Getting?"

"You know what I mean," he laughed. "You're getting really strong."

"Coming along," I admitted, rolling off and lying beside him. "Apart from little jobs here and there for your uncle, I've pretty much been working out six or seven hours a day up at the camp. Sit ups, pull ups, kayaking. I've been watching taekwondo videos to try and refresh what I know, but I really need to find a class. I started rock climbing lessons last month."

"Rock climbing?"

"You know, so I can be a better cat burglar. Scaling walls and picking locks, and such."

"Well," said Nick. "I don't know about scaling walls, but I can set you up with some lock pick lessons."

"Really?" I was psyched. "Marty's got me a little gadget for electric locks and keypads, but I really want to know how to do a tumbler, old school, you know?"

"Is this what everyone talks about after sex?"

"Oh," I teased. "You don't like to mix business with pleasure?" I raised my hand up in front of my face and studied my scar. It was a bad habit, and when Nick turned his head to me I quickly dropped it back to the bed.

"Now that you mention it," Nick offered, "Uncle Elgort does have something for you. Something big."

"Big? Really?" I sat up and straddled him again, excited. "So far it's just been a few surveillance jobs. Not very exciting, but I'm trying to keep a low profile. Being dead and all."

"Yes. Some breaking and entering, I think. Your friend Martin's toys will come in handy. Can you meet him tomorrow morning?"

"Yes, of course!" I bounced up and down with excitement, making the mattress creak.

9

Diamond White

"What do you think of this bed?" asked Nick, propping himself up on his elbows.

"Not bad," I said with a shrug, looking around the Shelby Furniture showroom. "Let's try that one over there next," I said, pointing to one with a big brass bedstead. "Or bunk beds!"

I awoke the next morning in Nick's townhouse, which was just next door to the furniture store. We decided it was probably not good for Margaret or Don to find us sprawled across the merchandise.

I sat up and looked around for Nick, who was just coming in the front door with a bag of pastries in one hand and a tray of coffee in the other.

"Morning, early bird," I said, snatching a croissant.

"Not in the bed please," he admonished. "Crumbs."

"Oh please," I huffed, but I got out of bed and put the croissant on a side table. I found my underpants and bra and put them on, then picked up my dress.

"Crap," I said.

"What's the matter?"

"I didn't bring any other clothes," I bemoaned, holding up the sexy green dress.

"So?"

"I can't go to a 9 a.m. meeting, with your aged uncle, in this! It'll look like the morning after."

He shrugged. "It is the morning after."

"Nick! I want him to respect me."

"Elgort's a lot more liberal than you might think. But if it bothers you, we can get there early and you can borrow something from wardrobe."

"Thank you," I said, and pecked him on his scratchy cheek. "I'll just get this on and go to the bathroom, then I'll be ready to go."

Diamond White

"Hang on a minute," he said, setting down his coffee. "I have a birthday present for you." He reached into his coat pocket and pulled out a small brown paper bag.

"But my birthday's in April," I said. "Not that I'm complaining. I love presents." I shrugged my way into the dress and sat on the edge of the bed, facing him.

He handed me an Illinois driver's license. The name said Riley McKay, and the photo was an edited version of one he had taken of me last night after dinner. It was flawless.

I leapt across the space between us, nearly spilling his coffee.

"Thank you," I beamed. "It's perfect!"

"I'll get a passport done this week. But at least now you won't have to put your Wrigley disguise on every time you want to go somewhere."

Georgette Wrigley was the identity I had been using ever since I was wanted by the police in April, for a crime I didn't commit. It came with a long black wig, and the need to apply makeup every time I wanted to go out.

Nick stood and drank down the rest of his coffee in one long gulp.

"You've been dead twelve weeks, and with the short hair you look pretty different from the Officer Riley photos that were circulating on the news back then. Plus your nose seems different. I think it's probably safe to ditch the wig and make-up."

"That's a relief," I sighed. "I'll miss Georgette, though; she was so much smarter than I am."

"That makes no sense, whatsoever."

"Maybe not," I shrugged. "You'd have to be someone else for a while to understand what I mean."

I walked into the nearby bathroom and looked at my face in the mirror. He was right, my nose was permanently crooked, the result of being caught in an

11

explosion that also split my head open. I also had a huge scar on my scalp, though it was completely covered by my hair, thank God.

"I'll be right out," I called over my shoulder. "Can I use your toothbrush?"

"Absolutely not!"

"You'll never know," I said, and closed the door.

Thirty minutes later, we were in the workshop on the top floor of the Shelby Furniture building. It was a fantastic place, filled with antique furniture and rugs, old roll-top desks, computers, photo equipment, lights, and clothing—racks and racks of clothing.

I found some gray dress slacks and a dark blue blouse that hid my black bra. I was trying on jaunty fedoras when a basket full of leather gloves caught my eye. I picked up a nice black pair. Hmm. On a workbench, I found some cotton batting for stuffing recliners, and used some of it to fill the ring and pinky finger of the left-hand glove.

"What are you doing?" asked Nick, coming up behind me and making me jump.

I pulled on the gloves, and held up my hands to him, as if in surrender.

"See?" I said. "Ten fingers!"

He frowned. "I understand you're sensitive about your hand—"

"No," I stopped him. "That's not it. I mean, yeah, but also, eight fingers are pretty conspicuous. My success often depends on fitting in—being unremarkable. Missing fingers get noticed, believe me."

He took both my hands in his, and squeezed them.

"You are remarkable," he said with a melting smile, then looked down at my hands. "Hey, that's not bad," he added, pinching the fake fingers. "A little soft. Let's try adding sand, in two little connected beanbags, so it can bend at the joint."

"Perfectionist!"

"Good morning!" cried a scratchy voice from the other side of the loft.

Uncle Elgort was making his way across the intervening space, one hand on the arm of Nick's older brother, Don. Elgort was in his mid-eighties, but had the gleaming eyes and strong voice of someone a decade younger. At one time, he had run a good part of the criminal activity in Chicago, but these days the Shelby family dealt mostly in finances and fake documents. And furniture, of course.

Don was ten years older than Nick. They looked remarkably alike, apart from the grey hair streaking along the sides of Don's head, and the crow's feet around his eyes. Unlike Nick, he was clean shaven and as I noticed when I gave him a brief hug, he smelled of cologne.

"I'm happy to see you alive and in one piece, my dear," said Elgort, giving me a hug.

"The same to you," I said, with my best smile.

He leaned back and looked me up and down.

"You're wearing some of our clothes..."

You know that thing they say about redheads blushing all the time? It's true.

"Umm..."

"No matter," he said quickly, to save me more embarrassment, "but why the gloves? Are you planning to rob a bank?"

"That's up to you," I replied with a grin.

He chuckled, and motioned to the round table that stood in the middle of the floor. We all took seats around it, just as the door opened and Margaret came in with a tray of coffee, which she set in the middle of the table.

Diamond White

"Anything else, Uncle?" she asked, turning to the old man.

"No, thank you. That's lovely," he said in a warm voice.

Margaret departed the way she had come. She was in her late sixties, if I had to guess. A cousin, or cousin-in-law, of Elgort. Family of some kind. A bit plump, with greying hair. Her matronly look was deceiving, as I knew she had her finger on the pulse of everything that went on in the building. She probably had tapes of Nicky and I testing out the mattresses on the third floor last night.

"Kay?"

"Huh?" I had been daydreaming about last night.

"Cream?"

"No, thank you, Don."

He replaced the cream on the silver tray, and then drew a notepad closer to himself, took out and put on a pair of reading glasses, and cleared his throat.

"Jared Dexter," he began. "Do you know who that is?"

"I'm sorry," I admitted. "I don't."

"No reason you should, I suppose," interjected Nick. "He tends to work behind the scenes."

"Exactly," continued Don. "Jared Dexter is one of the most powerful political operatives in Chicago. Probably in the whole country. His methods are not always above board, but he has managed to keep his hands clean— never any evidence of wrongdoing, even as we've seen multiple officials, even governors, go to jail."

"Is he working for the mayor?" I asked.

"As a consultant," Don continued. "We don't think the mayor has any idea what Dexter is up to. Dexter's working, we believe, with a Mexican drug and arms cartel."

"My God, that sounds a lot more serious than political malfeasance, which, frankly, I've come to expect in Illinois. How do you know this?"

Diamond White

Don sighed. "We aren't even sure, not one hundred percent. He came to our attention last year when we found his firm's name on documents lobbying against the funding of BUILD and other violence-mitigation programs in the city. Meanwhile, another one of his interests is pushing for harder police tactics, more paramilitary gear, more weaponry."

I sat up straighter. "How does he do this and work for the mayor?"

"He's very subtle," said Nick. "In fact," he added with a chuckle, "you'd pretty much have to be Eldon to figure it out."

"Well," said Don, "my skills are prodigious, but in this case, what he's doing isn't that different than what half the legislature is demanding. The rise in violence over the last few years, I believe, coincides with a glut of cheap, available guns on the street, and the simultaneous over-militarization of the police."

"And Dexter sells to both sides?"

"Oh no. Nothing that obvious. I'm not even sure what he gets out of it. Political pressure, perhaps for a party change in the mayor's office and in the statehouse. Money, surely, but I haven't figured out how yet. He doesn't handle any of the arms deals directly."

Uncle Elgort had been sitting quietly during this briefing, but now he slammed his palm on the table.

"I want him stopped! And that's what we are going to do."

"Umm, I don't want to sell myself short, but disrupting an international drug cartel seems a little bit out of my league. Last week you had me trailing a notary public." I hid behind my coffee cup.

Elgort looked at me with a pronounced seriousness.

Diamond White

"I don't expect you to stop him, Miss Riley. I will stop him. But I need more information, and I think you and your friends can do a job for me."

While Don poured more coffee, Nick got up and walked to one of the workbenches. He returned with a statue, about fifteen inches high, made of a dark brown metal. It was a woman, or young girl. The sculpture began at her head, and cut off at her waist. He set it on the table.

"This," Don began, "is a —"

"Degas!" I interjected.

He raised his eyebrows at me.

"What?" I retorted defensively. "I go to the Institute. Sometimes."

He tilted his head.

"Oh, you mean the interrupting. Sorry."

I locked my lips with an imaginary key.

"This," he began again, "is a copy of a statue. Made by me."

I whistled in appreciation.

"Thank you," he nodded. "We all have our skills. It's based on one of many studies that Degas did in preparation for creating the "Little Dancer, Aged Fourteen" sculpture that stands in the Art Institute. The same room currently holds several of these studies."

I looked at him, wide-eyed and attentive. I had no idea where he was going with this, but I loved watching him talk about his craft. It was sexy as hell.

"A similar sculpture sits in Jared Dexter's office. It can be seen quite clearly during a TV interview he gave last month about the upcoming mayor's race."

Uncle Elgort leaned forward again.

"I want you, Miss Riley, to break into Dexter's office, and replace his sculpture with this one, into which we

16

have placed a listening device. He must not, of course, know that you have been there."

This sounded good!

"It's a bit harder than it sounds," cautioned Nick, who could see the excitement on my face. "The office is on the top floor of a downtown skyscraper, which is only a big deal because the first three floors house the Chicago office of the Department of Homeland Security."

My smile drooped a bit.

"It's not that bad, you'll just want to be a little more careful than your usually very careful self," he hastened to add when he saw my reaction. "Dexter's office has electronic keypad security, an opportunity for you to test out Mr. Martynek's abilities. Other than that, you'll have to do your own recon and build a plan. Don's got a set of building plans you can take with you."

I finished my coffee and looked around the table, my gaze resting on Elgort.

"That all sounds good, I guess, but what does this have to do with the Shelby family?"

Uncle Elgort met my gaze.

"I've done a lot of bad things in my life," he began. "Things I'm not proud of. Violent things." He sighed. "But, they were done to create control. Yes, for my own benefit, and for my family's benefit, but the side effect of that control was peace, at least in certain parts of the city, for a period of time. This man," he jabbed his finger at the statue, "this man sows chaos, for personal gain. He profits on the destruction of young people, young poor people. Minorities. Teenagers."

His voice was strong with anger now.

"So many young people dying. In our city. I'm not going to stand for it."

Diamond White

Elgort sat back in his chair, and I could think of nothing witty or clever to say, so I smartly kept my mouth shut. For once.

3

"Ruby, what are we doing here?"

"Do you enjoy using my cabin as your private training facility?"

"Yes, of course, but—"

"Do you appreciate all I've done for you the past six months?"

"I gave you a million dollars!"

"True, but this is different. It's personal."

"I'm on board. For you, I always am. I just want to know what we're doing."

We were sitting in her car, parked on a leafy street in Evanston, intently watching a small house across the street. Ruby, in the driver's seat, was watching through binoculars, while I sat in the passenger's seat eating carrot sticks. Why can't potato chips be high protein and low fat? How 'bout it, science?

"We are here," she said, still looking through the binoculars, "to assault a police captain."

"What?"

"See! I knew you would be objecting." Her Czech accent always strengthened when she was riled up.

"I'm not complaining, I'm just, um, mystified."

Ruby put down the glasses and turned to me.

"Look, this new identity of yours. My retirement. We are to become like Batman, no? Righting wrongs by working outside the law?"

I winced.

"You make it sound really ridiculous...but, yeah. Sort of."

"These jobs you've been doing for Shelby. They don't seem very virtuous."

"Those were just practice!" I objected indignantly. "I gotta ramp up to being Robin Hood. I don't want to get clocked my first time out."

19

Diamond White

"I just don't think these Shelbys are on the same page as we are."

"You know," I said, putting my hand on her shoulder. "I might have agreed with you until yesterday."

"When you began having sex with the young one?"

"Not because of that!" Man, she was really on a roll tonight. I knew I shouldn't have told her. "Having sex with someone doesn't mean I believe they are virtuous. I can like bad boys, too, you know."

Ruby laughed. She actually laughed at me.

"What's that mean?" I demanded.

"You are funny. Making me laugh."

"Why?"

"Because you stole the money. You bought the leather pants, and that silly motor scooter."

"It's a motorcycle. Sort of. A really small one."

"My point is that you are still Miss Pollyanna. I mean that in a good way," she said, talking over my objection. "You want to be very tough girl, but at heart, you want to do the right thing."

"Okay," I sighed, crunching on a carrot. "So you're right. Whatever. I owed a debt to Uncle Elgort, regardless of whether I approve of what he does. But this time, Ruby, he's got a proper job for us, and it's really about stopping bad guys. Big, bad guys."

"Excellent," said Ruby. "That's what I'm in this for. Otherwise I would have taken that money and gone to the Riviera or some such."

"I know."

"You can tell me about this new job later, let's go get Captain Haines."

Captain Lawrence Haines ran one of the precincts on the north side of Chicago. It was an affluent area with not much crime, not many guns, not a lot going on. Haines wasn't a crooked cop. He wasn't taking money from drug kingpins or burying evidence. No, Captain Haines was just an asshole.

Two weeks ago, he had been charged with sexual harassment and two counts of sexual assault for cornering a young police officer in the women's bathroom and making unwanted advances, followed by equally unwanted touching.

A week ago, all charges had been dropped and he was reinstated, with no reason given. Sometimes the internal workings of the Chicago Police Department were maddeningly opaque, not to mention prejudiced and unfair. The incident had barely garnered a mention in the newspaper and would be forgotten completely within a week. By everyone except Ruby, that is.

The officer in question was named Ellery Park, an American born in Chicago to first-generation Korean immigrants. Ruby remembered processing the paperwork for Park's transfer from one of the downtown precincts to Haines's outfit. Top marks in school, top marks at the academy. As a result of Haines's reinstatement, Park had quit the force, and Ruby was pissed. The city needed more women in top law enforcement positions. It needed more women like Ellery Park.

Ruby handed me a ski mask and got out of the car.

"Really? Ski masks?"

"I'm sorry, I haven't sewn our superhero costumes yet. Put it on. It will go with your silly black gloves."

I put it on and got out of the car.

"Will you make me a fancy cape?"

"Make your own cape. I'm your operations manager, not your mom." She reached back into the car and pulled out her cane.

"Woah," I said as we crossed the road and entered the shadowy side yard of Haines's house. "With that attitude, you're either getting into character or you've got low blood sugar." I looked down at her cane. "You don't think the cane might be a distinguishing characteristic when it comes time for the captain to file an incident report?"

"I'm not worried. Who would suspect I would be involved in this? Plus, it's my weapon."

"Your cane is a weapon?"

Ruby stopped and turned to me. Grabbing the handle of the cane with one hand and the shaft with the other, she pulled them apart to reveal the beginnings of a long blade. It glinted sinisterly in the moonlight.

"A sword?" I hissed. "You bought a sword cane?"

"Well," she whispered defensively, "you're so sensitive about guns, I thought..."

"I'm a little goddam sensitive about swords, as well," I shot back, holding up my gloved hand to remind her of my missing fingers.

"Right. Sorry." She re-sheathed the sword.

"You're not planning on cutting any body parts off Haines, are you?"

She gave a low, menacing chuckle.

"Now that you mention it..."

We approached the back door with caution. No sign of dogs. The house was dark, apart from one light in a room at the front. I reached into the small backpack I was wearing, and took out a little yellow plastic box that looked more or less like a stud finder. Stud finder—that name always cracked me up.

I held it up to the side of the house just to the left of the doorway, pushed a button on the side, and slowly moved it in a widening circle until there was a small beep and a light on the top turned green. I'd have to talk to Marty about getting rid of the beep. It's not helpful when you are trying to be a ghost.

I marked the spot on the wall with my finger, and swapped the alarm finder for another small gizmo. This

Diamond White

one was dark grey and unbelievably heavy. It felt like one of the ten-pound weights that I used for bicep curls. Probably the magnets in it, or the power source. I placed it on the spot and pushed and held the trigger mechanism. It made a deep, resonant, but fairly quiet buzz, and then went silent.

Meanwhile, Ruby was cutting out one of the four small window panes set in the wooden door. She used a piece of duct tape to make sure the pane came out into her gloved hand rather than falling into the kitchen and smashing on the linoleum floor.

I nodded to her and she reached through to unlock the door from the inside. It swung open without a squeak, and we entered the dark house. I looked briefly to my left and confirmed that the alarm system hung powerless on the wall, completely shorted out. Score one for Technology Acquired, and their clever CEO, Marty Martynek.

We were in one room that was both kitchen and dining room, divided by a countertop that jutted out from the wall. The light was dim, which probably was a godsend, as the general vibe coming off the place was "Divorced, Living Alone." Ruby set the window glass carefully on the kitchen counter, then motioned down the hall where light was spilling from underneath a closed door. We made our way silently down the hall, stopping to listen carefully at the door. I thought I heard voices, but realized it was the low blathering volume of a television. I eased the door open silently, and we tiptoed in, Ruby gripping her cane tightly.

The room was empty. It was a sad little bedroom with a double bed, a dresser, and men's clothes strewn all over the floor. It didn't smell that great either. I checked the closet while Ruby looked under the bed. I examined the television and realized that both it and the beside lamp were connected to a timer at the outlet, one of those that you set to turn things on and off periodically when you are out of town.

I gave Ruby a dirty look over my shoulder, but then realized I was wearing a ski mask, so she probably didn't pick up on it. It would have been nice if she had made sure he was home before we dropped by. Oh well.

"Let's get out of here," I suggested, and we headed out of the room and back down the hall toward the kitchen.

When we passed the bathroom off to the right, I caught a movement in the shadow out of the corner of my eye. As I turned, a hard kick caught me in the side and knocked me against the wall and to the floor. I leapt back to my feet, but a dark figure had already burst past me and vaulted down the hall, pushing Ruby from behind. Ruby tripped over her cane, and the intruder tripped over Ruby, both of them tumbling into the kitchen.

The assailant was dressed in black, and like us was wearing a ski mask. He was quicker to get on his feet than Ruby, but Ruby's no fool. Instead of trying to get up, she swept her leg hard, catching the guy by both ankles and taking him back down to the floor.

I used the opportunity to jump over Ruby and come down elbow first with a move I had learned not in the dojang, but from watching World Federation Wrestling with my dad. This guy was quick, however, and was halfway up when I made contact. My momentum took both of us rolling across the ratty carpet and into the kitchen counter. The assailant gave a high-pitched yelp as we hit.

All three of us scrambled to our feet, facing off with hands raised to fight. Finally, in the moment we all took a breath, I managed to get a good look at the masked intruder. Masked intruder! How stupid of me; this wasn't Haines, of course. He wouldn't be wearing a mask in his own house, and the person was about a foot shorter than Haines. Shorter than me. And the noise they made when we crashed into the counter. I looked them up and down as they stood facing Ruby and I, favoring one ankle but still holding a strong defensive fighting stance. The form fitting clothes, on closer look, gave away a slim but decidedly female form.

"Where's Haines?" she rasped, ragged of breath, at the same time I demanded, "Who are you?" though I had a pretty good idea of her identity.

"Haines isn't here," said Ruby in disgust, leaning heavily on her cane.

Just then, from behind us in the shadows of the living room, came the unmistakable sound of someone cocking a shotgun, followed by a deep growling voice.

"Who says I'm not here?"

4

Haines stepped into the room and flipped on the kitchen light. It glinted off the long barrel of the shotgun that he was pointing at me. The woman I assumed was Ellery Park (who else would be breaking into Haines' house?) looked over her shoulder, saw Haines, and said, "Fudge."

Honestly, that's what she said.

"Against the wall," Haines barked, "all three of you."

We did as he said, lined up against the exterior wall; I could feel the cool night breeze coming in through the missing window pane.

"Jesus," he snorted. "Amateurs. Women! Park, you are going to prison for this, and your friends, well, them I might just shoot. But you, I want you to suffer through this indignity."

Ruby and Park both took a step forward, but stopped when Haines raised his shotgun.

"I'm not here," said Park, pulling off her ski mask. Long, shiny straight black hair fell down her back, almost to her waist. Her dark eyes were flashing with anger, and her face was flushed red. "I'm at an ACLU meeting in Deerfield with two close friends who will vouch for my whereabouts."

"These your two close friends?" Haines sneered, motioning to Ruby and me. "What if I just shoot 'em right here? Nobody's going to blame me, shooting intruders in my own kitchen."

Ellery Park's face faltered for a minute.

"Actually," she admitted. "I have no idea who they are."

"Bull," said Haines in disbelief.

Ruby took a step forward and poked Haines in the chest with her cane. It was an insane move and I gasped in fear as Haines batted it away, leveling the gun straight at her head. Undeterred, Ruby poked him again.

Diamond White

"Listen, Captain Assgrab," she growled. "I don't know who your friends are, and how they got your case thrown out, but I don't like the way you treat women." She gestured to me with her free hand and added, "And my friend doesn't like you either."

"Yeah," I said. I had no idea what her play was, but I winced when she once again poked Haines in the chest with her raised cane. Thankfully, he didn't shoot her. Instinctively, he reached out and grabbed hold of the cane in annoyance.

This, apparently, had been Ruby's play, because as soon as he had a firm grip on the cane she dropped to one knee, pulling the blade from its sheath. Spinning as she went down, she slammed the blade into his left leg just below the knee.

The shotgun went off, but it fired into the ceiling because Park had stepped forward as Ruby spun and brought both hands up under the barrel to force the gun up and away. When Haines screamed in pain she grabbed the gun and twisted it out of his hands, turning it on him as he hit the ground, rolling in agony.

Through the entire exchange, I hadn't moved a muscle. I just supervised. That's what leaders do, right? Oversee?

Clearly Ruby's sword cane was not a Hattori Hanzo sword, because it did not cut Haines's leg off. Not even close. It was a pretty good gash, though. Come to think of it, where the heck did she buy a sword cane? Not something you generally see at Marshall Field's. Maybe that's why they went out of business. Not a big enough sword inventory.

I was drifting. Time to focus. We had no idea if Haines had called for backup, so we had to move quickly. I opened my pack and took out the duct tape. Haines

Diamond White

screamed and thrashed as I wrapped it around his bleeding calf.

"Hold still, jerkwater," I said as I taped his legs together while Ruby sat on him. I secured his wrists behind his back, and then wrapped some tape around his head several times, enough to cover his mouth and keep him quiet.

"We gotta go," Ruby warned.

"Who are you?" asked Park, and I realized we had maybe just made her life worse rather than better. That can happen when you try to help. Still, gotta try, right?

I didn't answer, but instead opened a drawer under Haines's counter and pulled out a serrated steak knife. I then opened the drawer next to it, which was the drawer in every house that holds elastic bands, twist ties, menus, etc. I found a red Sharpie. It would do perfectly.

Park was starting to shake now, coming off the adrenaline. Ruby put her arm around her shoulder and led her toward the back door.

"We're nobody, honey," she said, and led her outside.

I straddled Haines on the floor, sitting on his chest and grabbing his hair with my bad hand. I banged the back of his head on the linoleum floor, hard enough to make him see stars.

"Hold still," I hissed, and with my right hand I placed the point of the steak knife in his left ear. "Don't move, or I will pop your eardrum, and if I'm not careful maybe stab you in the brain. Got me?"

His eyes rolled in fear, but he stayed still.

"Good. While you can still hear, listen to me. I am a ghost. I don't exist. But Park is real, and has a real life. Any of this blows back to her, and I promise you I will visit again. Your alarm system doesn't matter, your shotgun doesn't matter. I will visit you in the night while you sleep and you will never wake up to even know I was there."

I removed the knife and banged his head on the floor again.

"Got it, big boy?" I asked. He nodded.

"Good." I took the cap off the marker and wrote "Girls Rule" in big red letters on his forehead, then I stood, kicked him hard once in the ribs, and left.

Outside, I could hear sirens making their way toward us. I skipped across the street and climbed into the car.

"About time," said Ruby, who pulled away from the curb as soon as I closed the door. She had already removed her ski mask, and her sweaty face shone in the streetlight. I pulled mine off too, glancing out the back window as we headed down the street.

"Where's Park?" I asked.

"I sent her home," she said, turning onto McCormick. "Told her not to do any more stupid stunts like that. The girl's got a future."

"Did you tell her who we are?" I asked.

"*Ano,*" she nodded, "I told her we were Charlie's Angels."

I laughed. "She's twenty-three years old, she probably has no idea who that is."

Ruby laughed as well.

"Thank you, Kay, for coming with me."

"That was a total cluster, Ruby."

"Actually, I thought it went pretty well."

"It's okay," I said, looking out the window as suburbia slid by. "But if it's all the same to you, I think I'll be in charge of planning the Dexter job ."

We rode in silence for a few minutes, until I gave a low giggle.

"What?" she said, looking over at me.

"Sword cane," I said, shaking my head.

5

With tremendous effort, I reached up inch by inch, until my chalky white fingers found their grip on the little outcropping. I used my newfound leverage to pull myself even higher, my toes searching for purchase. I looked up. I was going to make it! I was only about five feet from the ceiling!

I completed the climb, touching the ceiling with my left pointer and middle finger before leaning back and letting the automatic belay lower me to the ground. Halfway there I passed Marty, who had been stuck in the same spot for about fifteen minutes. When he saw me go by, he gave up with a groan and followed me down.

Ten minutes later we were sitting side-by-side on a bench, legs sprawled out in front of us, drinking Gatorade and watching the other climbers. The place was packed, and ranged from families with kids to a few hardcore bearded guys with topknots. I'd had a few classes, then done a lot of extra work on my own. I had explained to my instructor, a chipper woman named Akilah, that climbing had been recommend as physical therapy for my hand, after a car accident.

Akilah was tall, with ropey muscles in her long arms. She made everything look easy, when it was damn hard, but even so I was coming along pretty well.

"Don't worry," Akilah had told me, "we'll have you playing the piano again in no time."

"Wow," said Martin, between slurps of his drink. "That is really hard. Thanks for inviting me out, Kay. I've done nothing for the past three months but work. I've gained at least fifteen pounds."

"Riley," I said.

"What?"

"Call me Riley, especially in public."

"Right. Right," he said. Catching on. "Call me CEO Martynek."

"Oh please," I sneered. "How's it going, anyway? Money was supposed to make your life easier, not harder."

"I know, right?" However, his eyes lit up with excitement when he began to describe his business. "We have the whole top floor of the building. You should see the view. Plus, I've rented a warehouse out on West Diversey for the R&D guys. You should see it, it's awesome. I was out there yesterday just flying a new drone around—inside!"

"That's great," I said, slightly distracted watching one of the instructors giving a lesson. The guy was in great shape, with long sandy-blond hair and sunglasses pushed up on the top of his head. He was great looking, but not really my type. I tried to picture Nick in tight Lycra shorts and climbing shoes, and laughed.

It was so strange. I was drawn to Nick, and his intellectualism and creativity. Despite having been a cop, I had always eschewed the precinct gym rats who spent all their time preening. Now, I was finding myself in the gym or working out seven days a week and it made me look at the people there differently. Sure, there were prima donnas, but there were also people getting in shape, people rehabbing from terrible accidents, and people for whom staying fit was just part of their lives.

I tore my eyes away.

"That alarm killer thingy. Totally worked, by the way."

Marty jumped right off the bench and pumped his fist in the air.

"Fantastic! I'm so happy!" He plopped back down, exhausted again. "Tell me all about it."

By the time I finished the tale, he was frowning, a deep crease between his dark eyebrows.

Diamond White

"Kay. Um... Riley, I don't like you involving my aunt in these capers. It's dangerous."

I sat up and looked at him incredulously.

"Were you not listening? It was all Ruby's idea."

"I know, but when you go along with it, you just aid and abet her."

"You try stopping her!"

He sighed. "I know what you mean, I do, but look at you," he said, gesturing his hand up and down at my body.

I looked down at myself.

"What?"

"You're killing it, Riley. You must have lost twenty pounds since April, and you scaled that wall like you've been doing it for years."

I straightened up and sucked my stomach in a little. I liked the sound of this. "Go on."

"You're not a kid, but you're not fifty-three years old, either. You're transforming yourself into an athlete, and a fighter, but Ruby is never going to be that. And that's dangerous."

I deflated, slumping my shoulders and looking away from him. He was right.

"Don't take her on jobs with you, Kay. Help her out. She's got these Robin Hood ideas and she wants to exact some justice, that's great. Help her with that, but keep her out of the line of fire. Please."

I stood and stretched my arms high over my head, then centered my feet and bent at the waist, putting my palms on the floor. I let the tension flow down my arms and into the mat, breathing out the tension before straightening back up again.

"You're not wrong, Marty. I'm not sure how to stop Ruby when she has her mind set on something, but you're not wrong. I'll think about it. I also think maybe we should get some cameras for the perimeter out at the cabin."

"Why," he asked in alarm. "Has anything happened?"

"No, no. Nothing like that. I've got to start planning a job and it's going to be the real deal. It made me realize that this whole crazy idea—doing jobs that punish the bad guys—is really starting to happen. I was worried that Elgort was just humoring me, but if this job goes wrong, we would be in big trouble with some very dangerous people. It would be prudent to be safe, and that starts with the cabin, and with your properties as well."

Rather than frightened, he looked eager. Kids.

"It's really a big job, huh?"

"It is. I'm going to need your help on the technical side."

"I live to serve," he said, bowing.

I tilted my head at the wall.

"Want to go up again?"

"Not a chance in hell."

6

An hour later, after one more trip up the wall, followed by a shower and a change of clothes, I was whipping down the Edens Expressway on my new friend, Gromet.

Gromet was a bright-red Honda Grom, a small motorcycle, which fit me fine. No Harley for me, just something light and fast. Very, very fast. I zipped through traffic like a leaf on the wind.

I'd learned from the surveillance work I'd been doing that a car can be a liability when you must move quickly, or stop quickly. You can't be circling the block looking for a parking place while your target saunters off along the sidewalk.

The only problem with Gromet was that, in spite of my intentions, he attracted a lot of attention. The little bike was so damn sexy that everyone looked twice whenever I sped by. I was thinking about asking Nick to paint it a more muted color and rough it up a bit, so that no one would look twice. But that didn't seem fair to my little baby Gromet, I thought, and patted its gas tank with my gloved hand. It's possible I was becoming attached.

Then I was thinking about Nick, which was a mistake because suddenly there was a siren behind me. Just a blast to get my attention, but it startled me so badly that I nearly lost control and launched over the guard rail.

I looked down at the speedometer. Crap. That's what I get for daydreaming. I shifted down and slowed the bike until I came to a complete stop in the breakdown lane. I shut the bike off, rocked it up onto its stand, and then took off my helmet as the police officer stepped out of his cruiser.

As I turned to face him, my heart leapt into my mouth and sweat flooded my armpits. It was Dale Murphy. We had been in the same precinct as rookies, ten years ago. A lot had changed since then.

Diamond White

Dale, for instance, was a good thirty pounds heavier, and it wasn't his hair that was adding to his weight. His scalp gleamed in the afternoon sunlight, the dark hair on the sides and back of his head shaved close.

Wow, did I have a crush on him that first year, but he hardly even noticed me. Or did he? We were about to find out. This was going to be a test of my new look, and my new credentials.

"Can I see your license and registration, ma'am?" he asked.

I set my helmet on the seat of the Grom and made a show of running my hands over my butt.

"I'm sorry, officer, I forgot. These leather pants don't have pockets. Let's see..."

I zipped my black leather jacket down slowly, and without removing my gloves I managed to pull the documents from the inside pocket and hand them over.

I looked him straight in the eye. It was now or never. Different hair, crooked nose, sexier clothes. I deepened my voice a bit and spoke with a slight Southern accent.

"I'm sorry, officer. I only just got this motorcycle, and I didn't realize just how fast I was going." I batted my eyelids, because in for a penny... "It's just so incredibly exhilarating!"

"Yes, Mrs...McKay—"

"It's Miss."

"Pardon?"

"It's Miss McKay."

"Right, Miss McKay."

I shifted my weight from one foot to the other, causing my leather pants to creak audibly, even over the noise of the passing traffic.

He looked down at my pants, then hastily looked away, then down at my license again.

Diamond White

"I don't have a record," I told him. "I only just got it. I haven't really had a chance to get in trouble yet. You can check!"

He handed me back the documents.

"That's okay ma'am, just see to it that you stick to the speed limit from now on. We don't want you getting into any trouble. Not without a police officer around."

"Like you?" I drawled.

"Exactly. It's for your own safety. We wouldn't want anything to happen to someone as pretty as you."

"Thank you, Officer..."—I leaned into his personal space to examine his name tag— "Murphy."

"You have a nice day, now, ma'am," he said, and turned back toward his cruiser.

Three minutes. In three minutes, he had said more to me on the side of the road than he had in the whole year we worked in the same building. I kicked a rock with my boot, and turned away from him as he drove past and pulled back on to 94.

In that moment, I held two conflicting emotions. One was regret that I hadn't gotten in shape and dressed better years ago. The other was anger that it made a difference. For a second I wished that all men would spontaneously disappear from the face of the earth, then I put my helmet on and got back on my bike.

"Not you, Gromet," I said to the little motorbike, which I had decided was a he. "You can stay."

Surprisingly, my lock-picking lesson was taught by Uncle Elgort himself.

"Ahh, those boys," he said dismissively, waving a hand. "Nick has the hands for it, but he is more interested in his art. Plus, he would be a distraction to you, and it takes utter concentration. Eldon, he is all computers these days. All the research, the finance, the deal-making. All computers these days."

Diamond White

I blushed at his reference to Nick, but he didn't notice. We were back in the top floor loft of the Shelby Furniture building, sitting at the well-worn table where I had first told him about my problems. It had only been about four months ago, but it felt like a lifetime.

Elgort was wearing his normal suit and tie, with highly polished brown leather shoes. He always looked like he had just stepped out of 1952, but it suited him. Added to his dignity. I hated to see old men sitting around in sweat pants. It just looked sad.

"The hard skills, they are disappearing. Because who wants to rob a lock box when you can just push a button and move funds from London to Switzerland to Monaco to the Caymans?"

"I like the hard skills," I said.

"I know you do," he said, taking my hand and tracing the calluses I had from climbing. "I like that about you. You do things up close, without all the layers in between." He dropped my hand and wagged his finger at me. "But be careful. Up close is difficult, dangerous."

"Easier to get caught," I added.

"Easier to get confused," he countered. "Look at the military, these days. Like playing a video game." He pursed his lips. "Pww pww," he said, making a shooting motion. "So detached. No accountability. No soul."

He wiped his mouth on his sleeve. "And since then, other things. Things not wars, but like wars. On the street. In back rooms, where violence is real!" He slapped his palm on the table. "Where you own your actions, and they make you question every step. And make you regret..." His voice faded, and he looked off to the side for a moment. Then he looked me in the eye.

"You and the no guns. I get it. I admire it. It's one of the things I like about you."

"Thank you."

Diamond White

"But be careful," he admonished, rising from his chair to his feet. "A choice like that is an easy one when you are alone. But when you must defend others, others you love, and you don't have the tools to do it. What then?"

He turned on his heel and walked toward the far end of the warehouse.

"Come," he beckoned over his shoulder, "I have a lot to teach you."

Yes, sensei, I bowed.

7

I was washing dishes in Ruby's sink a few nights later
when Ellery Park knocked on the cabin door. Needless to
say, it was a surprise. We were miles from Chicago, down
a back road through a forest that led to this little cabin
with its own yard and a dock. Ruby's little slice of fishy
paradise, though I hadn't seen her fish at all since moving
in. For my part, I had been doing a lot of kayaking. I
suppose I could swim here, too, but I liked doing laps in
a pool. Inside. Something about a lake made me always
think tentacles were going to reach up and grab me.

I opened the door, looked Ellery up and down, then
stepped back to let her in.

"Is Ruby home?" she asked politely.

"Sure," I grinned. This girl was something. I held out
my right hand.

"I'm Ellery Park," she said, in her timid voice.

"I'm Georgette Wrigley. Ruby will be down in a
minute. Can I get you something to drink?"

"Just water will be fine, thank you."

"How about iced tea?"

"Yes, sure. Thank you."

I went to the kitchen, stopping at the bottom of the
stairs to yell up.

"Ruby!? Someone is here to see you!"

A minute later Ruby clomped down the stairs. She
took them one at a time, favoring her bad leg. She
walked into the living room and looked at Park.

"Okay," said Ruby with a shrug. "I knew you had
talent, but two days, that is damn efficient."

"I'm sorry to do this, Mrs. Martynek, but it was just so
strange. I couldn't let it go." She was wearing jeans and a
light jacket, with a white t-shirt underneath. Sensible
shoes. She carried a handbag big enough to hold three
or four bowling balls. She set it on the sofa and then sat

next to it as I came in from the kitchen. "I couldn't figure out why someone else would have it in for Haines, unless he had assaulted other women, but I couldn't find any proof of that, just a few rumors. So why would you be there except to punish him for what he did to me, and why would you do that?" She wound down her speech, the nervous babble dying out.

"Here's your iced tea," I said, handing it to her with my damaged hand.

It was something else to watch understanding dawn on her face. First, she stared at my hand, as people do. Then her impeccable manners kicked in and she averted her eyes away from the hard pink scar tissue, looking instead at Ruby. Then, finally, a look of wonder crossed her face and she turned back and looked at me, studying my face. Women weren't as easy to fool when it came to looks.

"I recognize you from somewhere."

"I used to be a cop."

"You quit?"

"No, I died."

She looked back at my hand again.

"You're..."

"Bingo," I grinned.

"But you're..."

"Nope." I plopped down on the sofa next to her. "Not dead."

"But they only found..."

I waved my damaged hand at her again.

Ruby sat in the easy chair in the corner of the room.

"Miss Park. How exactly did you find me?"

Ellery was still staring open-mouthed at me.

"They said you killed those people!"

"Then they said I didn't, to be fair."

"But then you were dead!"

42

Diamond White

"Boo."

"*Divenka*!" said Ruby, snapping her fingers. "Over here."

Ellery turned to look at Ruby. She was a lovely young girl with a serious face. Not gorgeous, per se, but pretty, and clearly a woman of many talents. You could almost see the wheels of logic and speculation working behind her eyes.

"Now, how did you find me?"

"Oh, it wasn't hard," she said, bright with the topic. "The only halfway-reasonable explanation for someone to show up at Haines's was the same reason I was there: revenge. Who would care about what he had done to me, apart from my family? And you were obviously not my family.

"It had to be a cop. A female cop who didn't like that Haines was getting away with being a slimeball. On our way out of his house, you told me to go home and stay far away from Haines. I could tell you had an accent. Eastern European of some kind. And the cane. I thought maybe you were injured in the line of duty. Yesterday was my last day on the job. I took advantage of the employee database and looked for on-duty leg injuries for officers with Eastern European backgrounds."

"Eh," said Ruby, "not bad. You must have got quite a few hits, though, yes?"

"Yes," said Park, leaning forward. "But when I read that you had been involved in the Red Riley Bombings, I knew it had to be you. Only a bad-ass like you would go after Haines."

Ruby sat up straighter and smiled. I don't know if Park was flattering her on purpose, but it was working like a charm. Then her smile dropped, just as suddenly.

"If it was so easy for you, perhaps Haines will come to the same conclusion."

43

Diamond White

"Oh, I don't think so," said Park. "One, you didn't say much in the kitchen that night, so he probably didn't catch the accent. Two, he's a moron."

We both laughed at that.

There was a silent moment, during which Ellery Park looked around the room, taking in the odd mixture of fishing décor and exercise equipment, tactical gear, and vases full of wildflowers.

"So," she said, bringing her attention back to Ruby and I, "what are you two doing way out here anyway?"

"Bass fishing?" I suggested with a shrug.

She laughed. "Yes, I'm sure that's it exactly."

By the time Ellery left, the three of us had ironed out a plan. I needed some extra help on the upcoming Dexter job, and wanted to leave Ruby out of it. Park was off the force, and didn't quite know what she wanted to do next, but liked the sound of sticking it to someone who had been supplying many of the guns that were flooding the street.

I was worried that she would be a stickler for the rules, and not want to participate in the kind of illegal entry we were planning, but she had no qualms about it at all. Kids these days. Or maybe, just maybe having your commanding officer push you against a bathroom wall and put his hands all over you had a disruptive effect on your respect for authority.

I thought about what she had said about Ruby, and the Red Riley Bombings. Maybe I should get a t-shirt that said, "I survived the Red Riley Bombings" across the chest. It was strange to be famous and to be dead.

Regardless, she was a sharp kid, and would be a big help. I had been struggling to come up with a plan that would work with just me, but I had made a promise to Marty.

Diamond White

I thought about what Uncle Elgort had said about protecting the people you cared for. But this wasn't like that. This was just business. Park was a hired henchman—henchwoman—for this job only. She would be paid commensurate with the risks, and then we would go our separate ways.

After she was gone, I locked the door and turned the alarm on. Ruby had already started toward the stairs for bed.

"Well," she said over her shoulder, "That went well." She put one hand on the bannister and started her slow progress up.

"What do you mean?" I asked, bewildered, before realization dawned. I crossed to the bottom of the stairs, glaring up at her with my hands on my hips.

"You knew she was going to be at Haines's house that night!"

Ruby stopped on the landing and turned back toward me.

"Of course I knew."

"You weren't avenging her, you were recruiting her!"

"Of course I was," said Ruby with exasperation, and continued up the stairs.

Yes, sensei, I bowed.

I looked across the yawning chasm between the top of Dexter's building and the top of the building nearest it, where I was standing in the chilly night wind. The nighttime view of the lake from up here was outstanding, but with it came the high wind, biting even in September.

I was wearing black tights and a black turtleneck, with a tight black sweater over it and a black backpack. A black knit watch cap covered my red hair, and of course my black Doc Martens completed the black ensemble. How much more black could I get? None. None more black.

On top of Dexter's building was a huge antenna. That was my target, and even an inexperienced pilot like me should be able to handle it. I thumbed the levers on the control box, watching as Marty's drone tilted a bit to the left, a bit back to the right, and then leveled off at head height. It was a pretty good-sized drone. It had to be, because it would be dragging about sixty feet of industrial hemp twine behind it.

I glanced down over the edge of the building. Mistake. Major mistake. Down below was a single-lane service alley between the two buildings. Twenty-five feet, max. Tom Cruise always made it look so easy. At least I wasn't jumping out of a plane.

Looking back across, I sent the drone on its way. Almost immediately, it veered about ten feet to the right. It was a constant fight to control it in the blowing wind, and even with our nice, heavy DJI model, it was a fight I was losing.

"Give it here," demanded Ruby, holding out her hand for the controller.

"Wait," I complained, "I've almost got it." The drone dropped suddenly out of sight below the edge of the roof line. I leapt forward to keep eyes on it, managing to

Diamond White

level it and bring it back up to our height, then set it back down on the roof without smashing it into either of the buildings.

I handed the controller to Ruby.

She examined it for a second, peering down through her reading glasses to look at the two small levers on the control box.

"It's like the Super Mario Brothers, no?" she asked.

I shook my head in amazement.

"I just, can't even..." but Ruby wasn't listening. The drone lifted up and flew smoothly across the alley, around the base of the twenty-foot antenna, and back over to us, where it landed neatly on the pebbled roof next to my feet. Step one, done!

We now had a continuous loop of hemp twine stretching from my side, around the antenna, and back to me. I picked up a coil of quarter-inch clothesline, and tied it tightly to one end of the hemp. Then I pulled on the free end, watching the clothesline cross the empty space between buildings, holding my breath as it somehow slid around the antenna without getting snagged, and came all the way back to me again. Step two, easy-peasy!

Next up was twenty meters of dark blue Mammut climbing rope, because climbing rope is metric for some reason. I snipped off the hemp, and connected the climbing rope. This proved much harder to pull across and around the antenna because of the accumulated weight, but with Ruby helping, we got it done.

Ruby took one end of the climbing rope and I took the other, and we backed up on either side of a large air conditioning unit. We joined the ends together in a series of very secure knots. Step three, done.

So far, so good. Now all that was left was the summoning of courage. I tested the rope by tugging on it three or four times, until it became obvious that I was

Diamond White

just stalling. Then I clipped my climbing harness to the rope and climbed up onto the low wall surrounding the edge of the roof.

"Give me the statue," I said to Ruby.

"I don't have the statue."

"Oh well," I said, turning from the edge. "No statue. Shucks. Guess we better go home."

Ruby frowned at me. "It's in the backpack. On your back."

"Oh really? I didn't realize..."

"Go!" she commanded. "And don't look down," she advised. "And good luck."

It took seven minutes to shinny across the rope, hanging upside down with my legs wrapped around it. I was no Tom Cruise which, frankly, was just fine with me. However, there was no way I could leave this way if anyone was chasing me. I'd be a sitting duck. Then I'd be a falling duck. Then I'd be a dead duck. There was no doubt about it, I would have to stick to the plan and leave through the front door.

I lay for a moment on my back on the roof of Dexter's building, letting the adrenaline drain from my body. Controlling my breathing, I lay still until suddenly the drone flew right over me. I sat up quickly and looked back across to Ruby, who was standing on the edge, controller in her hand.

"What are you doing?" I hissed at her.

"It's fun. And now I have the video of your little circus performance. I thought you'd want to see it, when we got home."

"It has a camera?" Cool.

"Yes, you didn't see it hovering next to you when you were crossing?"

"Frankly, Ruby, my eyes were closed. Now get the rope and get out of here. I'll meet you at the bunker."

Diamond White

The drone buzzed uncomfortably close to my head on its way back across the alley. I glared at Ruby, but she had already turned away. A moment later the rope was untied and she hauled it back over to her side. I looked down the eighteen stories to the street and shuddered. So far, so good. Not dead. That was really my only barometer of success.

I crossed to the door for the stairs, took off my backpack, and pulled out the alarm silencer. It did its job with that satisfying bass thrum, and then it was time for the locksmith to do her job. That's me. In this scenario, I'm the locksmith. I hope.

I pulled out the little billfold of tools Uncle Elgort had given me and went to work on the deadbolt. I tried, and failed, for four minutes until finally I felt the mechanism turn to the side, and I gently pulled the door open. Yes!

The lights in the stairwell were on, but I figured they were on all the time in a building like this. I put my tools in the backpack, and slipped it back on. Entering the stairwell, I eased the door shut behind me. It was the kind with a crash bar and a sign that said, "Emergency Exit Only: Alarm Will Sound." Goes to show what you know, buddy.

From a holster on my hip I drew my new tranquilizer gun. I was pretty proud of it, though I had yet to try it on a real person. It's amazingly hard to find volunteers.

Inside my boot was a switchblade, just in case. My cap was the kind that doubled as a ski mask, and I rolled it down over my face before starting silently down the stairs.

It was 11:30 p.m. My primary concerns were security guards and cleaning crew. I wasn't really expecting anyone to still be working in Dexter's offices, but you never know, so it was best to be overly cautious. Prowling the halls of an office building in the middle of the night

Diamond White

gave me unpleasant flashbacks to that eventful night in the Farnham Building, when Carter Blalock exploded in front of me, changing my life forever. It made my skin crawl and I wanted to run, but I took a deep breath and forced myself to take it slowly and carefully.

As a result, it was 11:42 before I made it down to the fifteenth floor, the floor that held the offices of Jared Dexter and one of his companies, Good Policy, Inc. I looked at the name plate on the door and snorted. Good Policy. I already hated this guy and I hadn't even met him.

The office door had a keypad, but Marty's gizmo made short work of that. I entered, then re-armed the door behind me.

I moved quickly through the open floor plan of the darkened room until I found the door to Dexter's private office. It had its own keypad, which was soon rendered inert as well. I'm not sure how it worked, but the machine managed to disable the part of the alarm that recognized a breach, without showing the unit as malfunctioning. I had acquired some excellent technology from that boy.

While I was tempted to do some searching in Dexter's office, to see if I could find anything good for Uncle Elgort, I was already behind schedule, so I headed straight for the statue on the back credenza. I swung my backpack off and pulled out the copy. It was a perfect match.

Nicky, you are a sexy genius.

I made the switch and then looked around for the bathroom. Seems Dexter didn't have a private one in his office—man of the people—so I exited the room, closing the door and reactivating the alarm.

On the other side of the cubicle farm I spotted two doors, spaced about ten feet apart. Maybe offices, maybe

51

restrooms. I made my way quickly to the other side of the vast space.

Yup, two dark wooden doors, one marked with an M and one with a W. I was tempted to use the men's room, just because I was all alone and I could, but I chose the women's instead. Guess I'm not as daring as I like to think I am.

I went to the sink and pulled off my ski mask. Oof, that felt good. I took off my backpack again, and from the front compartment I retrieved my Georgette Wrigley black wig and a crumpled grey suit coat and skirt. The skirt looked pretty good over the tights and boots. It would do.

Two minutes later, I was looking at my alter ego in the mirror. Not bad. I liked the dark hair; it was a nice change from my usual red. I reached out and was just about to turn on the faucet to splash some cold water on my face when I heard a toilet flush through the wall.

Damn! Someone was in the men's room! Or was it somewhere else in the building?

Through the wall I heard a forced-air hand dryer kick on. Yep, I had company.

I slung the pack onto my back and quietly exited the bathroom, dropping to a crouch and working my way back across the cubicles toward the entrance. As I approached the door I heard the hand dryer quit and the squeak of the men's room door.

I dropped to my knees in front of the keypad, hurrying to pull the gizmo from the backpack. Damn, there wasn't going to be time! I rolled to the side and into a cubicle, squirming behind the chair and under the desk as the man approached the office door. From my contorted position, I could see shiny black shoes and black pantlegs with piping down the side. Security.

Diamond White

I eased the tranq gun from its holster, but I would have to show myself to get a clear shot, and the whole point of the job was to be unnoticed. Reports of a break-in would likely cause a search of the entire office. Who knows, they might even sweep for bugs and then the game would be up before we ever got started.

I heard four beeps on the keypad as the guard opened the door and let himself out. Phew.

I lay on my back and contemplated the meaning of life for a count of sixty before I crawled out from under the desk and made my way carefully out of the office. I smoothed my suit jacket and made sure it covered the holster on my hip. I heard a door close at the end of the hall. I guessed that my unexpected friend was taking the stairs either up a floor or down a floor. When I was certain he was out of earshot, I pulled my phone from my backpack and pressed a preprogrammed number. It rang.

"Good evening, Department of Homeland Security, how may I direct your call?"

The voice was that of a chipper young woman.

"Can I have two orders of hotteok for delivery?"

"I'm sorry," the voice said, "but I believe you have the wrong number."

"That's too bad, because I'm really ready for some Korean takeout."

I hung up, and made my way down the hall to the elevator. The security guard was possibly several floors away by now, but I still bobbed nervously on the balls of my feet while I waited for the elevator to arrive. The décor here was expensive, with wall sconces and some nicely framed Manet prints on the walls.

Finally, the elevator arrived. The ding made me wince, but no one else was around to hear it. I stepped on and pushed the button for the lobby. I noticed there were no buttons for floors two through five—Homeland Security.

53

Diamond White

It went from six straight to the lobby. Looks like my hunch about the lower stairwells being off limits was probably true.

As I descended, I caught sight of myself in the mirrored wall. It was startling to see the raven-haired Georgette looking back at me. It had been a while since she had been out and about. I winked at myself, then took my backpack off and held it down by my side, so as not to interrupt the businesswoman vibe I was trying to give off.

I reached the lobby and the doors opened with a ding. I took a deep breath and strode out confidently, making a beeline for the metal detector and the street exit beyond it. I chanced a look to my left as I crossed the space, and there, seated at the guard's station, was Ellery Park in her dress blues. Instead of a Chicago Police badge, she wore a silver name tag and had a Homeland Security patch on the shoulder of her uniform. I raised my eyebrows at her and she nodded imperceptibly, motioning toward the floor with her eyes. I glanced down as I was passing her, and could see the legs and feet of a security guard sticking out from under her desk, but out of view of anyone on the street. I wondered if it would make the news tomorrow. Would Homeland Security admit one of their guards had been incapacitated? They would probably spend days quietly trying to figure out what the intruder had been after. No one would suspect Dexter as that target.

I walked through the metal detector and it shrieked to life. I knew this was coming, but I still jumped a foot.

"What's going on down there!" a voice barked from above.

I looked up and could see a large, florid-faced security guard leaning over the atrium railing. Walrus mustache, big gut. Clearly retired police. I waved up at him.

Diamond White

"Sorry, working late!"

"Don't move," he barked, but Park was already moving toward me with one of those metal detector wands in her hand. She kept her head down, so the guard up above couldn't see her face, and said in a loud voice, "Pardon me, ma'am, but I've got to check you out. Can you step over here please?" She took me by the elbow and pulled me closer to the door.

I looked up at the scowling man and shrugged, smiling. He grimaced and turned away.

Park kept moving me along until at the last minute she dropped the wand to the floor with a clatter and we both stepped out the front door and into the night. We sprinted across the street to where Grom was parked and threw on the helmets waiting on the seat, I pulled off the grey skirt, shoved it in the backpack, and hopped on the bike.

It was a tight fit with two, even though Park was quite small. I handed her the backpack and she put it on, then leaned close and grabbed my waist as the bike roared to life.

And then we were off, into the dark city.

9

No sign of pursuit from Homeland, but we'd only gone about three blocks when suddenly we were broadsided by another motorcycle. The driver, all in black leather, with a black helmet and mirrored visor, had come out of nowhere and actually swerved into us, shoulder first, to try and make me lose control of the bike. And I very nearly had. With the extra weight on the back, I over compensated and would have dumped it if Park hadn't leaned hard back toward the other cyclist. She grabbed the tranq gun out of my waistband but as she turned to use it the attacker sideswiped us. Park lost her grip and the gun clattered away. As the other bike began to pull ahead of us, Park lashed out with her foot and kicked the back of their seat. The girl had a ton of moxie. The driver had to adjust to regain his own balance, and in that instant I hit the gas and we were away. However, we had barely gotten up to speed when the assailant was back, suddenly level with us, the black motorcycle glinting under the streetlights. Where? How?

"Ruby!" I screamed into the headset built into my helmet. "I need you now!"

I banked the Grom hard onto North Fairbanks, heading south. It was midnight in downtown Chicago; the streets were still full of people and cars, though not quite as many as during the day.

I cut it too close and jumped the curb, Park hanging on to my waist for dear life. In my mirror I saw the pursuing motorcycle, a Harley, corner smoothly, arc out around a taxi cab, and pull back in behind us. I opened the throttle all the way, but the other bike was faster and was soon pulling up on my left flank. It was hard to drive and watch at the same time but when I felt Elle pulling hard on my waist I chanced a look over my shoulder.

Diamond White

The attacker was steering one-handed. With the other hand, he brandished a long sharp knife. Park kicked out with her foot to keep the biker at bay, but it was precarious. I tried to move to the other lane, but just then the traffic was keeping us boxed in. Our assailant had perfectly chosen the time to make his move.

Two more quick slashes from the biker. I winced, thinking surely they had done damage, but had to keep my attention on driving. A huge tug on my shoulder threw the entire bike off balance. Elle had a hold of the back of my jacket with one hand, with the other she was clinging to the backpack by a broken strap. No, not broken! Cut! The assailant, rather than stabbing Park, had sliced deftly through the two straps of the backpack, and was now trying to pull it away.

But Park wasn't letting go without a fight, though her left hand was surely going to lose its grip eventually. The biker had dropped the knife in order to grab the bag with his right hand. At least the danger of a stabbing was gone. Bright side!

Why didn't Park just let go of the backpack? It was just a statue. Let it go! I tried to shout to her, but she didn't have a radio in her helmet and the roar of the engine was too loud.

"Ruby!" I shouted again in panic.

I turned hard onto Grand, gunning straight for a mailbox standing on the corner. The old pick and roll; my Dad would have been proud. The other driver, unable to wrench the pack out of Elle's hand, was forced to let go and swerve, over the sidewalk and around a planter, sending people leaping out of the way. I pulled a hard left across oncoming traffic and raced down a side alley, trying to lose them.

I rounded the next corner, and couldn't hear over the roar of my own bike to know if we'd been followed. The

Diamond White

alley twisted to the right, got thinner, then thinner still, until finally it spit us out onto a thoroughfare. I shot straight across, miraculously avoiding impact with a green Honda Element, and continued down an even smaller alley on the other side that took us right past the *Tribune* building and onto Michigan Ave.

I screeched to a halt on the sidewalk, nearly hyperventilating with adrenaline. I could feel sweat trickling down my ribs under my turtleneck. I turned and grabbed the backpack from Elle, who was reaching up to take her helmet off when I spotted our adversary heading up the sidewalk after us. He must have come all the way up Grand and then spotted us exiting the alley.

I made a split-second decision and pushed Elle backward off the bike and onto her ass on the sidewalk. I snugged the backpack in front of me, between my thighs, and hit the throttle hard, still on the sidewalk and heading south.

It was possible that the assailant would stop and kill Ellery Park, but I didn't think so. They seemed intent on the backpack. A minute ago, I was urging Elle to let them have it, but now that they wanted it so bad my natural stubbornness kicked in, and I wasn't going to give it up without a fight. There had to be some important reason for him to want it so much.

And so I was hurtling down the sidewalk of the busiest street in Chicago, even at this time of night. As I approached the river, I spotted a gap in the oncoming traffic and turned hard across the lanes, over the divider, and fishtailed onto the southbound lane. I chanced a look back to see if I was being followed— I was—and then I opened it up full as I hit the DuSable Bridge and crossed the river.

Without Park on the back, I was going much faster, but I couldn't shake my mysterious pursuer. Where the

Diamond White

hell had they come from? After our walk-off play from Homeland Security, Park and I had gotten out of there quickly; who could have followed us?

"Kay, where are you!"

It was Ruby, at last, in my ear.

"Thank God, Rube. I need help. Some maniac is trying to take me down and steal the backpack!"

"That doesn't make any sense!"

"And yet..."

"Where are you?"

"I'm south on Michigan, where the heck are you?"

"I'm on Wacker."

"Damn it, I'm already past you."

"I'm coming!"

"No, stay there, meet me at the end, under Lake Shore Drive."

"Got it. Out." And she was gone.

A flash in my rearview caught my attention as the other rider pulled in right behind me. Damn, I was never going to outrun them, and we would start attracting the cops any minute.

I feinted right like I was going to turn onto Washington, then swerved back left, timing my move between a bus and a bright yellow car, crossing the oncoming lane and then downshifting quickly as I jumped the curb and entered the plaza in front of the giant mirrored bean sculpture. If you've never been to Chicago, you have no idea what I'm talking about, but trust me, it's real.

I glanced briefly at my funhouse reflection in the side of the bean, then hit the brakes harder, putting my left foot down for balance as the back wheel swung around. I throttled hard again and headed off across Millennium Park, tooting my horn and willing people to get out of the way.

Diamond White

I finally attracted the attention of the police as I sped across the Great Lawn in front of the amphitheater. When I looked over my shoulder to see if I was still being followed—I was—I could see red and blue lights flashing back by the bean.

I cut my engine and lights and glided off the lawn and up onto the pedestrian bridge, hoping Mr. DaftPunk would lose me in the dark.

No such luck, and now I was slowing down from the bridge's incline. I popped the engine back on, the headlight terrifying a couple making out against the railing, and drove as fast as I dared along the winding bridge until it brought me back down to ground level and into Maggie Daley Park.

I seemed to have opened up a little lead with my bridge trick. When I looked behind me I couldn't see the other bike. I grinned as I approached the corner of Lake Shore Drive and Monroe, only to look right and see the cyclops headlight coming straight up the street.

Okay, this was getting exhausting, but I was almost at my endgame. I sped across Lake Shore Drive and onto the Lakefront Pedestrian Trail that started in front of the yacht club, turning left and heading north again.

There weren't a lot of people walking, but the roar of Gromet's engine was all the warning they needed to get out of the way.

DaftPunk make a smart move and cut across the grass to my left, catching up to me as we reached the docks stretching out to our right, into the lake. I hunched over the handlebars, which had the added benefit of better protecting the backpack between my legs.

He pulled to within five feet of me as Lake Shore Drive began to rise on cement pillars beside us, readying to cross the Chicago River. I swerved under the elevated road and ducked as something hurtled past my head.

Diamond White

It was the drone, and it hit DaftPunk straight in the face! He never saw it coming. I swerved to the right and back onto the grassway as the other motorcycle fishtailed wildly before falling, the driver pulling his leg out and up to his chest just before the machine would have crushed it. Driver and bike slid wildly across the grass, separating as the rider hit a stand of thick bushes. The bike missed the bushes and continued forward, finally scraping across the cement walkway and stopping right on the edge of the river.

I pulled to a stop, panting, as Ruby's Subaru pulled up on the breakwater access road and she lowered her window.

"Nice flying," I gasped as I pulled my helmet off and hung it on the handlebar. I threw the backpack into the back of her car.

"*Sakra!* Are you okay?"

"I'm fine," I said, climbing off my bike and putting down the kickstand. "But you better get out of here, I don't want you seen."

"What are you going to do?"

"I'm going to get some answers," I said, and started toward the bushes.

"Be careful," Ruby called as she drove away, doing what I asked her to do for once.

I approached the other biker cautiously, to see the leather-clad figure crawling slowly out of the bushes. I took a running start and kicked him hard in the stomach, the upward force flipping him over onto his back. I straddled him, a knee on each bicep, ensuring his arms were immobile. Then I pulled off the black helmet.

"Shit, it's you!"

"*Mierda!* It's you," wheezed Selena Salerno at the same time.

Diamond White

"Are you okay?" I asked, then checked myself. Was I crazy? What did I care?

"Can't...breath..." she croaked. I took my weight off her. She beat her right hand against the ground, trying to inhale; she'd really had the wind knocked out of her.

My brain was doing cartwheels. Salerno. Here! Chasing me! Was it coincidence? Her former boss was in jail, because of me. Was it revenge? How did she know I was alive?

At that moment, Salerno gave a huge, rattling gasp. She breathed again and rolled over on her side, trying to get up on all fours.

"You're, alive!" she gasped. "Impressive."

Well that answered one question. She had indeed believed I was dead. So what was she doing chasing me? Here was the conundrum: I wanted answers, but I had no way of subduing Salerno—no cuffs, no duct tape, and any minute she would have her faculties back. Once she was on her feet I wouldn't be able to beat her in a fight; even in this state she'd make short work of me. Behind me, I could hear the sound of sirens coming closer. I decided I'd better get out of there. I could only hope that Selena would keep my secret safe. But who would she tell that I was alive? The police? Aldo Frances?

I ran to her motorcycle. It was a beautiful black Harley Street. I felt bad as I reached down and, grabbing the frame, levered it over the edge of the promenade and into the river with a splash.

I heard Salerno groan behind me and turned to see her up and staggering toward me, like an angry but gorgeous zombie. I side-stepped her and ran back to my bike; she was still too winded to follow. She stopped, hunched over with her hands on her knees. Before I started the engine, I opened the storage container and pulled out my cell phone.

63

Diamond White

"Give me your number," I called to her, but she was lumbering toward me now, and picking up speed.

"Never mind," I said, and threw the phone in her direction. I put my helmet on and climbed on the bike. "I'll call you."

I put Gromet in gear and roared off toward Lower Wacker, stopping at the first streetlight to fasten the strap on my helmet.

Safety first, after all.

10

In the basement of Marty's building was a windowless office we called "the bunker." It had been a workspace for him before his recent windfall, and he still leased it, perhaps for old times' sake. I made use of it often when I was in the city. It was a two-room office, but it had a little kitchenette off the main room and a bathroom off the smaller one. Basically, an apartment without a shower, but you could get creative in the sink. I often did.

I was met at the door by El. I thought she might be mad at me for ditching her, but she seemed thrilled to see me still alive. She stepped forward to hug me, then thought that might be too forward, so she awkwardly slapped me on the back and dragged me into the main room. It was still decorated the way Marty had left it: old 1980s movie posters, a few couches, two folding tables with three computers and monitors on them. A big corkboard had index cards pinned all over it, outlining our plan to use a drone to cross the rooftops and switch the statue. The plan didn't mention Selena bloody Salerno anywhere in it!

I looked at Ruby, who was making tea in the kitchen. We stared at each other for a moment.

"Thank you," I said.

She shrugged. "You see? You need me in the field, still."

"Where did she come from?"

"Crazy," said Ruby, coming into the living room.

"Wait, she?" gasped Park.

I looked at Ruby. "You didn't tell her?"

"I thought I'd wait for you."

I walked past the kitchenette to the smaller room, with the bed in it. On the kitchen counter as I passed was the Degas statue. Unharmed. The little dancer's face stern in concentration. I stuck my tongue out at her.

Diamond White

I kept a dresser full of clothes here now. I wonder what Marty's girlfriends thought, if he brought any of them here. A quick wash in the bathroom sink and a new outfit, jeans and a bright orange t-shirt that said "Moxie" on it, and I was feeling better. I brushed my teeth quickly, too, to get the clammy taste of abject fear out of my mouth.

Back in the living room, I was halfway through telling El the thrilling "Tale of the Sexy Assassin" when the door opened and Marty came in.

"What the hell happened?" he blurted, giving me a bear hug, then turning to give a long embrace to Ruby.

Marty was twenty-four years old, and was now the CEO of his own booming tech business. He had a better haircut now, but he still looked young and rough, which is, I suppose, exactly the look that you want for a wunderkind tech millionaire if you want the media to love you. And the media loved Marty. He had beautiful blue eyes and dark wavy hair, and his enthusiasm was contagious. When he was interviewed on the Chicago news, everyone around him looked like they were carved from tofu. He was huge on social media, where he had rocketed from obscurity to celebrity over the summer based on an app game about fire hydrants and meter maids called "Red Zone White Zone." Marty was a case study of the ways in which it took money to make money. He'd always had the ideas, but it was a deep investment in promotion since our recent windfall that led to his breakout success.

He let go of Ruby and turned to El. "Hello, small person, whom I don't know but trust implicitly because you are with Kay and Auntie. Welcome to the bunker!"

"This is Ellery Park, our new henchwoman," I told him. "El, this is Martin Martynek, CEO of Technology Acquired."

Diamond White

"Nice to meet you," said El. "I'm a big fan of your work."

"Oh," smiled Marty. "Red Zone?"

"No," she said, "the electromagnetic alarm disarmer. Brilliant!"

"Right. Right! I'm so glad I could be of use, and I'm so glad you're all still alive! Ruby told me there was a near-catastrophe, so I rushed right down. Also, I ordered pizza. It should be here in ten minutes."

"That," I said, plopping down on the couch, "is the best news I've heard all day."

I looked across at Marty, who was perched on the edge of the computer table.

"It was Salerno."

He went pale.

"What? No! How?"

I shook my head.

"I wish I knew. It's got to be a coincidence, right?" I ran my half hand through my hair. "When she saw it was me, she was surprised. I mean really surprised—no way she was faking that."

"Okay," grunted Ruby. "So, we don't know why. What about the what?"

"Come again?"

From her spot next to me on the couch, she gestured to the statue on the counter. "She clearly wanted the statue. Why?"

"How did she even know you had it?" asked Marty.

"Hmm," I hmmd. "Based on what I know about Selena, she very well might have planted a camera somewhere in the room. She could have seen me take it."

"But you weren't Georgette, yet," countered Ruby. "She would have recognized you."

"Maybe," I admitted.

Diamond White

Meanwhile, Park, who was sitting on one of the high stools at the counter, walked over to the statue and turned it upside down. She picked a butter knife up from the countertop and started to pry at the bottom.

"What are you doing?" I asked.

"Well," she grunted, getting more leverage, "we hid something inside the statue we left in Jared Dexter's office, right?" We all nodded. "Who's to say there wasn't something hidden in the statue that was already there?" And with that the bottom of the statue flipped free, flying across the room and hitting the *Blade Runner* poster. "Voila," she said, shaking the statue until a small black felt bag fell out onto the counter.

We all gathered around as Elle picked up the little bag, loosened the string, and tipped a handful of diamonds onto the counter. They shone a pure, perfect white.

"Golly!" she exclaimed.

11

I gasped, and Marty gave a low whistle. It was like a fairy tale; no one ever expects to see a pile of diamonds, not in real life. There had to be forty or fifty of them, each the size of a small pebble.

"Golly is right," said Ruby. "This makes more sense now."

I groaned and slapped my forehead.

"What horrible luck! Of all the things we could've swapped out, we pick the one with the priceless jewels."

"I don't see how that's exactly bad luck," said Park, holding one up to the light and admiring its brilliance.

"Don't you see? We're supposed to be invisible. Our job was to plant a listening device, without anyone knowing about it. I think they're probably going to know about it when they check on their diamonds!"

"Which they must have already done," chimed in Marty, "if Selena was on your tail so quickly."

He opened his mouth to say more, but his phone chimed in his pocket. He pulled it out and glanced at the text message on the screen.

"Pizza's here!" he said cheerfully.

"I may have lost my appetite," I moaned.

"You know, Kay, that never happens to me," said Marty. "Not sure why."

He took two twenties from his wallet and handed them to Ellery. "Go meet them in the lobby, would you?"

"Why me?"

"Lowest on the totem pole," said Ruby, with authority. "Go."

As Park left, I looked back down at the diamonds.

"We'd better hide these for now," I said, pushing them back into a pile. Ruby picked up the little felt sack.

"Wait a minute," I said, reaching back into the pile to pull out one of the diamonds. "What's this?"

Diamond White

I held it up to the light. It wasn't a diamond. It looked a bit like a small watch battery, but on the bottom there was a tiny green LED.

"Let me see that," said Marty. I came around to his side of the countertop and gave it to him. He moved across the room to the computer table and picked up a little box covered with switches and lights. I followed him to the table, and we both bent over for a close look as he held the box above the doodad and flipped a switch.

There was a small beep. I frowned.

"Meaning?"

"Active electronics," said Marty.

"Like a battery?" I asked, but the tumblers in my brain had already turned, and I saw the answer bearing down on me like a freight train.

"No, more like a—"

"—homing device," I finished, already turning for the door.

"Park!" I shouted, running into the stairwell. I looked up just in time to see El hurtling backward down the stairs. She crashed into me and we both fell hard on to the concrete. I sat up as I heard boots banging down the steps toward us.

Salerno jumped the last three stairs and landed next to me, cocking her elbow back and into my solar plexus, knocking me back to the ground. She was wearing a close-fitting black tank top, which had probably been under her leather jacket. Her riding pants were rasped and torn from where she had slid across the concrete path and into the bushes.

Park jumped into a fighting stance, but she was no match for the Mexican. She went down under a flurry of kicks and punches, blocking maybe half of them, until she was on her back on the ground. Salerno gave Park one last kick to the ribs and she lay still.

Diamond White

"Park!" I yelled again, as Salerno turned on her heel and marched back over to me.

"You!" she spat, and her usual flirtatious grin was gone. "I liked that bike!"

Before I was halfway to my feet, she wrapped me in a headlock and dragged me over to the door of the bunker, slamming the top of my head straight into it, and causing stars to explode at the edges of my vision.

I clawed at her arm, but her grip was iron. She opened the door and dragged me down the hall and into the living room, where Ruby was leaning on her cane, her old police Glock in her right hand.

"*Hola*," said Ruby, and cocked the gun.

But Selena didn't stop. She barreled straight at Ruby, twisting as she moved so that I was between the two of them as a shield, straight-arming Marty as he rushed at her from the side. He staggered from the blow and fell into the computer table, scattering gizmos in all directions.

I tried to get a foot under me to relieve the pressure on my windpipe, but at that moment Salerno threw me forward and into Ruby's cane, knocking it, and her, to the ground. In an instant, the woman's right hand was locked onto Ruby's wrist, and with her left hand she released the magazine on the Glock. It fell to the ground and skittered across the kitchenette floor as Salerno twisted the gun from Ruby's hand and threw it across the room in the other direction.

Ruby rolled over and away, behind the counter, and I came up to my feet with a turn kick that should have taken Salerno's head clean off, but Selena was way ahead of me, blocking my foot with her forearm while sweeping my other leg out from under me. I landed hard on my back, and she was on me again: knees on upper arms in a reverse of our position in the park, just over an hour

71

Diamond White

ago. She leaned forward and put her forearm on my neck, pressing hard enough to obstruct my air.

"Don't move, computer boy," she said to Marty, without looking to the side. He had picked up a fallen lamp and was starting toward her, holding it like a club. "And you," she barked. "*Tia*. Get back where I can see you, or I break Red's windpipe."

Ruby came out of the kitchenette with her hands up, and Marty also stood down, dropping the lamp on the carpeted floor with a thud.

Salerno rolled off me in a move that was so fast I couldn't follow it, somehow dragging me up to a sitting position and then pulling me, by my short hair, to my feet. Her arm was around my neck again, this time from behind, and she pulled me close to her, backing up to the far wall, so she could see both Marty and Ruby at the same time. I could feel her chest rising and falling against my back, fast at first but then slower as the heat of the moment passed. Her bare arm was still firm against my neck.

I racked my brains for a plan that would keep her from killing me, and then after, my friends. Suddenly it came to me: Give her the diamonds!

"Give me the diamonds," hissed Selena, the moment I thought it.

"Sure," I croaked. "You can have them."

I looked over at the countertop, but the diamonds were gone! I panicked for a moment, then recalled Ruby gathering them up when the pizza arrived. Then I panicked again. Ruby. This was going to go really badly, I could tell.

"Ruby, give her the diamonds," I said.

"No." I knew it. Here we go.

Salerno tightened her grip on my throat. She had told me once that she didn't kill people, though I hadn't really

Diamond White

believed her. She had certainly caused people to die, but maybe that was just a moral backflip she used to help herself sleep at night. Regardless, the grinning, puckish woman from that time was gone. This Salerno was tense, and all business. Maybe I shouldn't have wrecked her bike.

Selena looked at Marty.

"Tell me where they are, or I kill her."

Marty still had his hands up, over his head, like in a stick-up.

"I honestly don't know," he said, his voice quivering. This was probably true, technically. He and I had been busy examining the tracking device when Ruby had hidden the diamonds. On the one hand, I admired his ability to lie—or misdirect— convincingly under pressure, on the other hand there was no need to put her threat to the test, not when my life was potentially on the line. I pulled hard with both hands on Selena's arm, but it didn't budge. The whole time a part of my mind was on Ellery Park, lying in the stairwell, possibly dying.

I looked back at Ruby.

"Ruby," I grunted. "This is silly. Just give her the diamonds. What's the point?"

Ruby just ignored me, levelling her gaze at Salerno. She held out her arms wide and turned a slow circle.

"You can search me," she taunted, "but I clearly wouldn't hide them on my person. I've put them somewhere safe, and this room, though tiny and poorly decorated, will take you too long to search."

"I will kill her!"

"I don't think you will," said Ruby. Great, psychoanalysis was just what we needed right now. "Besides," she shrugged, "if Kay is gone then there are more diamonds for me."

73

Diamond White

Selena snorted. "I don't believe that for a moment." She gestured at Marty. "You going to let me kill him, too?"

I bugged my eyes at Ruby. What was she stalling for? Did she think Park was going to save us? I wasn't even sure El was still alive.

"You are just stalling," Selena continued. "You think the *chica* in the hall will save you." Woah, jinx again.

Ruby's face turned dark and thoughtful.

"He is blood," she said, gesturing at Marty. "It would be a harder decision, but one I won't have to make. Security will be here any second."

Selena snorted, spittle going right on the side of my face. "That is ridiculous."

"It's not," said Ruby calmly. "We have tactical force, ever since someone tried to blow Kay up this spring. Tactical force, silent alarm. Full military response. They will blow down that door any minute."

"That's bull—" but she didn't get to finish her sentence, because there was a series of loud, popping explosions. I flexed my legs and slammed Selena back against the wall, breaking her grip in the confusion, grabbing her hand in both of mine and wrenching it backward.

She gave a low scream, and threw me off her, so hard I went over the back of the couch and onto the floor. I looked up and saw black smoke billowing across the ceiling. What the hell had Ruby done? My thoughts were shattered by an ear-splitting alarm going off. I got to my feet and looked around to see Selena crouched in a fighting stance, face to face with Ruby, who was holding her sword in front of her with two hands. She wouldn't stand a chance against Salerno, sword or no sword.

Suddenly, with a hiss, the sprinkler system came on, instantly soaking us all with lukewarm water. Ruby's hair

74

Diamond White

was hanging in her face, but there was a triumphant gleam in her eye.

"They are coming!" she taunted, with a laugh.

For a moment all was still. Selena and Ruby faced off. Marty stood against the wall, eyes ping-ponging back and forth between his aunt and his computers, which were getting wetter by the minute. I stood by the couch, examining Salerno, looking for a way to incapacitate her. I contemplated a flying sidekick at her back, but she seemed to have eyes in the back of her head, and I'd probably end up impaling myself on Ruby's sword.

Selena growled, a wolf in her frustration, and took a small step toward Ruby. Distant sirens joined in with the sound of the fire alarm, deafening in the small space.

"They are coming," Ruby shouted again over the noise.

Salerno howled, then turned and raced down the hall and out the door, gone in an instant.

"Park!" I shouted, running after her.

Ellery Park was still lying on the concrete floor of the stairwell, but she was moving, the water bringing her back to consciousness. I didn't see blood anywhere, so I reached down to pull her to a sitting position.

"No," cried Ruby, coming up behind me. "Don't move her; it might be her neck."

Elle groaned and turned her head toward the sound of Ruby's voice. She opened her mouth.

"Why is it raining inside?" she asked.

12

The next evening found me riding through south Chicago in a long black limousine. I still had a headache from the activities of the previous night. I had found a lime seltzer water in the limo's bar and was sipping it as I slumped in my seat.

I was wearing a black skirt, with a black silk shirt and a light grey Anne Klein jacket. Trying to make a good impression after failing my first big job for Elgort. I reached over and gave him the pouch of diamonds.

Uncle Elgort sat opposite me, dressed impeccably as always. Dark grey suit, white shirt, dark blue tie. A fedora rested on his knee. His grey hair was neatly trimmed and the streetlights shone in his spectacles as we glided down the street. He waved the pouch away.

"You hang on to them," he said. "Nicky will meet you. I want him to see about making some good replicas."

I put the pouch back in my pocket and stared out the window.

"I'm sorry," I said.

"No," Elgort said gently, as the car rolled to a stop in front of an old three story Victorian house, "you didn't fail at all. You did exactly as asked. Who could have foreseen this Salerno woman and her tracking device?"

Eldon, who was driving the limo, exited the car and came around to the passenger's side as a dark figure came slowly down the front walk from the house. Eldon took his arm and helped him into the car.

"Thank you, Don," said the old man, who turned his body and sank slowly onto the seat. Lifting first one leg, then the other, into the car, he added, "I don't move as fast as I used to."

"No worries, Sir," said Don, shutting the door firmly before moving back around to take his seat behind the wheel.

Diamond White

Uncle Elgort motioned to the man now sitting next to him.

"Miss Riley McKay, may I present Captain Alden Earl."

"Retired," put in Earl.

"Yes, of course," added Elgort.

"It's an honor to meet you, sir," I said, leaning forward to shake his frail hand.

Holy crap. Alden Earl was a legend in the police force, even though he had been retired for more than fifteen years. A rough-hewn product of the south side, he made good as a young black police officer who couldn't be bought. He was, or had been, a big man with wide shoulders. I'd seen plenty of pictures of him. Hell, there was even a statue of him in Ogden Park. He became a hero during the 1968 riots, after the assassination of Martin Luther King, and later that year at the Democratic Convention as well. Tough year, 1968, I guess, but this all happened before I was born. I'd kind of assumed Earl was dead, to tell you the truth.

What the heck was he doing with Uncle Elgort?

"Strange times make strange bedfellows," said Elgort, clearly anticipating my question.

"Indeed," agreed Earl.

"Captain Earl has been working with me on this project regarding Jared Dexter. He agrees with me that Dexter is somehow involved in the increase of guns flooding into the south side. I trust him, implicitly."

Hmm. You do, huh? I mused. But you introduced me as McKay. Interesting.

"So," I said, "you said on the phone that the surveillance was blown. I'm sorry."

"Don't be, my dear girl," said Earl. "Miraculously, they did not discover the transmitter until almost sixteen hours after you planted it. Apparently, this woman that you are tangled up with—"

Diamond White

"—Salerno."

"Yes, that's right. Apparently, Miss Salerno gave her initial report to Dexter over the phone. She was at the hospital having her wrist x-rayed. It wasn't until earlier this afternoon that she reported directly to Dexter in his office."

"So?" I asked.

"Well, she had chased you through the night, and at Martin's office she had seen the Degas statue on his kitchen counter. Imagine, then, her surprise when she saw the same statue still sitting in Dexter's office."

I snapped my fingers.

"Right. Dexter probably assumed we'd just taken the diamonds out of the sculpture and left it behind, but when Selena arrived at his office, she realized there were two."

"Exactly," confirmed Uncle Elgort. "It was then a matter of minutes before they found Eldon's little listening device and disabled it."

"So," I said, sipping my drink. "All of that for nothing?"

"Not at all," said Earl, his voice still deep and resonant despite his advanced age. "That morning Dexter spoke at length to a person in Mexico. We think he's our man."

Earl pulled a small notebook from inside his windbreaker, and flipped it open. He reached into his other pocket and took out a pair of half-frame reading glasses. He set the notebook on his lap and pushed the glasses he was already wearing up onto his dark, shiny forehead, put on the reading glasses, and then picked up his notebook again.

"Antonio Negron," he said at last.

"I'm afraid that means nothing to me," I sighed.

"That's the interesting part, Miss McKay. He means nothing to anyone in Chicago. In Mexico, he is a landowner and considered to be one of the wealthiest individuals in the country, but he has no connection to the crime rings or drug lords down there. None that we can find."

"Just like Dexter," I mulled out loud.

"Exactly," said Uncle Elgort. "You see the beauty of it. Neither of them with any criminal affiliation. No one to suspect them in the least."

"Which is why they were using a regular phone."

"Correct," confirmed Earl. "You only need to worry about what you say over the phone if someone is listening, and as far as they know, there's no reason for anyone to suspect either of them of anything."

I sat up on the edge of my seat. "Until you two came along and put it together. And Selena! She was in his office. She must connect to Negron somehow. That's our line."

"Yes," said Earl. "But she's a ghost. We have no idea how to find her, apart from surveilling Dexter around the clock. I've got some people on that."

"And," added Elgort, "I know a few trustworthy people in that part of Mexico. I will begin some quiet digging into Señor Negron."

"What do you want me to do?"

Elgort leaned forward.

"I want you to find the ghost."

"Easy," I said with a smile.

13

The limo rolled up quietly to the sidewalk. I got out, then leaned back in toward the two serious old men.

"Give me a few days to pull a plan together," I said. "I want to wait until Ms. Park can join me."

I closed the door and turned toward the little brick plaza where I had left Gromet, on the outskirts of the University of Chicago. There, leaning against the bike, was Nick Shelby, my favorite forger and artisan. My favorite artisan forger.

"Nice ride." I said as I approached. I took the diamond pouch out of my pocket and dangled it from my finger. "Trade you for it."

"It's a nice bike," he said, pulling himself up to his full height and taking the bag, "but it's not that nice. It's all yours."

He put the bag in his pocket and I put my arms around his waist, pulling myself in close and putting my head on his shoulder. I felt his arms encircle my back.

"I'm so glad you're okay," he said softly, and I nearly broke into tears.

I don't know what the experts say, but I'm not sure you ever become inured to extreme physical danger. Maybe athletes do, maybe firemen do. I don't think cops do. I know I haven't. It had been a rough twenty-four hours, between high-rise rope work, a high-speed motorcycle chase, and the invasion and destruction of the bunker.

My anxiety and self-pity dissolved into Nick's shirt. So much so that I just about dozed off standing there.

"Kay?" Nick prompted eventually.

"Huh? Oh, right. What next?"

"You should get some sleep."

"Is that an invitation?" I pulled my head back and gave him my best mischievous grin.

Diamond White

"Sure, if you don't mind giving me a ride."

"Actually," I caught myself, "I have somewhere to be. I need to go look at an apartment. With the bunker ruined, I need a place to crash when I'm not up at Nippersink."

"You can stay with me," Nick offered.

"I don't want to be an imposition. I think it would be better to have my own place."

"It's not an imposition," he insisted.

"I'm messy."

"I don't mind."

"I'd eat your food."

"It's good food."

"I'd use your toothbrush and not tell you."

"Ahhh..."

"Gotcha !" I said. "It's too soon. Plus, not entirely safe. For you I mean."

He stepped back, his hands on each of my shoulders, and looked into my eyes.

"Okay," he said, "too soon. But you are welcome there any time. Toothbrush or no."

I reached up and gave him my very best kiss. The one I save for special occasions. It went on a while, until someone walking past whistled at us.

"It's 10 p.m.," Nick said, breaking away. "How can you possibly have an appointment to see an apartment?"

"Oh," I said, nonchalantly. "I was just going to break in and spend the night. See how I liked the space. I hate realtors."

He raised his eyebrows.

"Really, really hate them," I repeated. "You want to come with me and test the mattress?"

He patted his pocket. "I think I better get started on this right away. Sounds like you and Uncle Elgort are on a time schedule."

Diamond White

"You know what they say: Early bird with the fake diamonds gets the scuzball politician and the psychotic gymnast assassin."

"Is that what they say?" He grinned.

"Verbatim. Still want a ride home?"

He started to walk off toward the campus, calling over his shoulder.

"I have to meet a friend at the chemistry lab."

"Is that a euphemism?" I called back.

He shook his head and kept walking. Laughing on the inside, I bet.

14

I woke up on a bare mattress, unsure of where I was. Neutral walls and ceiling, beige carpet. Oak dresser, high-end blinds, en-suite bathroom that looked marbly and bright from where I was lying. On the wall was a framed print of the Chicago skyline in silhouette. How original.

I stretched and sat up, leaned over and looked out the blinds. I was pretty high up; I could see the lake. Down below I could see North Halsted, full of cars all trying to get somewhere.

That's right, North Halsted, my prospective apartment. I got up and padded on bare feet into the stylish bathroom. Halogen lights, double sink. I peed in the toilet, cursing because there was no toilet paper. I leaned over and opened the cabinet under the vanity and lucked out. Three rolls stacked one on the other. I grabbed one and put it to use, also finding an unopened bar of soap but no shampoo. Oh well.

I took off my clothes and looked at myself briefly in the mirror. The redness around my throat was gone this morning, but there was still a good-sized mark on my right side where Park had hit me when she came hurtling down the stairwell. I leaned forward and looked at my face and chest. Yep, freckles still there.

It was a walk-in shower, so I unwrapped the soap and walked in. There were three(!) separate shower heads, and I was caressed with warm water from all angles. This place really sucked.

Fifteen minutes later I stepped from the shower and realized I didn't have a towel. Damn. I walked back into the bedroom. Furnished but no linens. That's what I get for not taking my towel with me everywhere I went. Sound advice.

I pulled the previous day's clothes on over my wet body, found my satchel and searched for a comb or brush. No luck. Well, that's the beauty of a short haircut. Disheveled is a style. I pulled on my shoes and jacket and slung the satchel over my shoulder. Grabbed my keys off the dresser and opened the door to the living room just as a someone on the other side of the door reached for the doorknob.

I was surprised, but she was more so, shrieking and stumbling past me into the room. I stepped out into the living room where her matching husband was looking out the window. An older, sharply dressed woman in strappy heels was standing in the open archway to the kitchen, leaning on the jamb and flicking through information on her phone. She looked up and gasped as I strode out.

The young woman recovered her balance and came back out behind me into the living room. Her husband turned at the sound and his jaw dropped open. I wound my way through the chic, boring furniture and down the beige hall to the door.

"Hey," said the man, finally finding his voice. He was small and had a little paunch to him, but a nice suit. Banker. Sits at work all day. Mrs. Banker was too confused to say anything, and Ms. Realtor couldn't stop me if she wanted to, not in those heels.

"This isn't going to work for me," I said, my hand on the doorknob. "This place has absolutely no soul."

I opened the door. "Also, you need some towels."

As I closed the door I heard the young woman say, "Ethan, who was that?" in a hilariously accusatory voice.

A half hour later I was sitting in Oz Park with a coffee and a scone. I had a strange craving for Mexican, but the Taco Joint wasn't open at 10 a.m., which was probably for the best.

I used to be a creature of habit, but becoming a ghost had changed me fundamentally. I found myself trying new and different foods, buying different clothing. I was

Diamond White

alone a lot—social media was dead for me—and in addition to all the exercise I was getting, I'd been reading more books and going to more museums and concerts.

I was lonely, but also raw and alive and ready to try new things. Living in a high-rise luxury apartment wasn't one of them, though. That was for sure. I was going to have to find an apartment soon, however. Preferably one with laundry.

I had a moment of fear when I realized that the realtor might have called the cops after I left. Did I leave any fingerprints? Nah, nothing was missing or broken; I doubt she did anything about it. Still, I should really be more careful.

I put down my coffee and dug around in my satchel until I found the burner phone I had picked up the day before. I checked to see if I had any messages; I had made quick calls to Elgort, Nick, Marty, Park and Ruby to make sure they could reach me if need be. My social media network—I could list my contacts on one hand. Well, on my right hand I could.

No calls.

I finished my scone, wiped my hand on my leggings, and dialed the number of my old phone. It was possible that she wouldn't answer, that she had thrown the phone into the river. But if she had it, she would answer. I had what she wanted.

Ring.

My biggest concern was Ellery Park. She had to make herself disappear, at least while Salerno was on the loose. That hadn't been the plan. She was a henchwoman for hire. She was supposed to be able to go back to her family and friends when she wasn't doing jobs for me. I wasn't trying to breed more loners, that's for sure.

Ring.

Diamond White

Ruby could clearly take care of herself, and Salerno knew nothing about the Shelby family, not as far as I knew, anyway.

Ring.

Marty was the only one out in the open, but he had stepped up his security heavily in the forty-eight hours since the mayhem in the bunker, and he had some clever little electronic surprises for anyone who tried to break into his office or house.

She answered after the third ring.

"Riley."

"*Hola!*" I said, in a big, cheerful voice. "How are you doing this morning, Selena?"

She didn't respond.

"Can you hold the phone okay?" I pressed on, lightheartedly.

"What are you talking about?"

"Your wrist. I was afraid I had damaged it so badly the other night, you might not be able to grip the phone properly."

"It's fine," she growled. "Did you call me to gloat?"

"'Cause I thought I heard a snap when I whooped your ass."

"You're a riot, *chica*. You're all only alive because I need the diamonds. Four of you! Against one. I barely broke a sweat."

"Funny about those diamonds," I said, maintaining a pleasant tone. "Ruby had them in her pocket the whole time!" I chuckled.

"*Ni cagando*! I should have killed her." Her accent seemed to strengthen with her anger.

"I thought you told me you didn't kill people."

"Usually, no, but for her I could make an exception."

88

Diamond White

"You know," I said, watching a woman push a jogger through the park, "strapping an exploding bracelet to a person is a little bit like killing them."

"I didn't push the button though, that was not part of my job."

"Wow. Moral relativism, much?"

"Things are dire, Riley. I need those diamonds."

"I need information," I countered.

"About Jared Dexter? I can do that."

"And about Antonio Negron."

"No, Riley," her voice hissed down the line. "How do you even know that name?"

"Not important," I said. "But I seem to have hit a nerve." The woman with the jogger bent over it and straightened up, holding an amorphous bundle of blankets to her chest. I assumed there was a kid in there somewhere.

"Forget you know that name, Riley. Trust me. You will wish you had never heard it."

"Is that who you work for?"

"Not on purpose."

"Is he your boss?"

"Nobody is my boss."

"Is he your dad? Dad issues."

Selena groaned on the other end.

"Disgusting. No, he is gross. And Mexican."

"You're not Mexican?"

"Of course not. Do I sound Mexican?"

"Ah..."

"I am from Chile! Isla Grande!"

"Okay, okay," I said.

"Mexican. Ha!"

"Can we get back on track here?"

"You don't want to get involved with Negron."

"Oh, you're my friend, now. Little sister?"

Diamond White

There was silence for a minute.

"Never mind, Riley. You can have what you want. Everything I know."

"When?"

"Tomorrow. I need to put it all on a thumb for you."

"Make it Friday," I said. "Millennium Park again. This time during the day. Lots of people around. Make sure I can see you, and I'll find you. Noontime."

"I don't like the sound of it, Riley. I show up, nothing but police. How do I know you'll keep your word?"

"I'm a ghost. I don't exist. I don't want the police around any more than you do. Besides, it's not like the police could ever catch you."

"You're right," she said.

Flattery will get you everywhere.

15

Valerie Archer was proceeded into the room by a large man in a black suit. He flicked on a few lights and walked swiftly through the living room and into the kitchen. Nothing. He moved into the bedroom, checked under the bed, got back to his feet with a soft groan, and then checked the closet.

"All clear, Miss Archer."

"Thank you, Stuart, that will be all."

"Yes ma'am, we'll be on the street all night."

She closed the door and locked it behind him. Her apartment was surprisingly small, for the Chief Operating Officer of Farnham, one of the biggest phone and data providers in the country. She likely had a house outside the city somewhere, and probably a classy little vacation home in Colorado, or the Bahamas.

At thirty years old she was a wunderkind, handpicked by Ferris Farnham to be his second-in-command. She was self-assured, almost regal, with deep brown skin and short, tightly curled hair. Her business suit was well-tailored to show off her shape without flaunting, and her jewelry was simple yet expensive.

She took the suit coat off and laid it over the back of the chair, stretching her arms above her head and then messaging her neck.

I was surprised at the high level of personal security, but then again, the whole escapade with the bombs was only three months ago. To me, it felt like a lifetime, since so much in my life had changed. I really was a different person now, in so many ways. For Archer it was probably still very fresh, and though the villain, Aldo Frances, had been apprehended, I could understand why those in powerful positions at Farnham would still be taking precautions.

Diamond White

As she moved into the kitchen and opened the fridge, I slipped out from behind the full-length drapes in the living room and crept up behind her. She was leaning over slightly, staring blankly at the shelves of food and drink, lost for a moment.

I felt bad: there was no easy way to do this, so like ripping a Band-Aid off, I did it quickly. I stepped my right leg between Archer's feet from behind, clamped my right hand over her mouth, and snaked my left hand up under her left arm and behind her neck in a quick half nelson. She tried to scream, but no sound came out. She tried to kick, but I kicked her right foot out to the side, throwing off her leverage. She tried to reach behind her head for my hair, but my short haircut gave her nothing to snag.

"Shhh," I said into her ear as I steered her out of the kitchen and into the bedroom. I kept our forward momentum going until her knees hit the end of the mattress and we both fell forward onto the bed. She made a quick move to throw me off, and she was strong, but I had all the leverage and I used it, pushing her face into the bedding. I removed my right hand from her mouth and snagged her right wrist as she tried to hit me, pulling it up between her shoulder blades as I sat on her lower back, releasing her from the half nelson at the same time.

"Don't scream," I warned. "I'm not here to hurt you."

She continued to thrash, but didn't scream. She must have realized that security was five floors down and across the street, sitting in a Ford Taurus and eating knishes from a bag. I levered her right arm a little higher up her back until I was sure it would be painful, and she began to settle down.

It was dark in the room, but I had cased it earlier. I knew there were two bedside tables and that neither held a gun. I knew there was a dresser full of very nice clothes,

Diamond White

and a walk-in closet with more of the same. The connected bathroom had all the regular things, but of a higher quality than most, as well as a man's razor, but since it was electric I didn't feel very threatened by it. Still, it reminded me that her boyfriend was a security expert and about fifty pounds heavier than me. I better make this quick.

I jumped off her back and the bed in one quick move, stepping to the bedroom door and closing it, I turned back toward her and leaned firmly against the only exit. I flicked on a switch next to the door that turned on the two bedside lamps.

Valerie Archer had rolled over on her back and was just sitting up when the lights came on. She rubbed her neck with her left hand while rotating her right shoulder around to get the feeling back into it.

"What the hell do you want!" she growled, as I stepped away from the door and closer to the light.

"I need your help," I told her. She looked at me in confusion for a second, at my hair and my face, and then as recognition dawned her big, brown eyes grew wide.

"You're..."

"Yup."

"But you..."

"Died?" I offered helpfully.

"But they found your..."

"Fingers?" I said, cheerily, waving at her with my left hand.

Her eyes caught what was missing, and her expression changed from wonder to revulsion.

"Oh, that's disgusting!"

"Thanks!"

"That you would do that, for money—"

"It wasn't quite like that."

93

Diamond White

She stood up and took a step toward me. I assumed a ready stance, but she didn't seem like she was preparing to spring at me.

"What was it like?" she asked.

"Well Frances had me wher—"

"No," she said, pointing at my hand. "What was it like to cut your own fingers off?"

Strange question.

"Actually, I had a friend do it for me. And it hurt like hell; in fact I passed out from the pain. But, I had been expecting to lose my whole hand, so, in a way, I was psyched."

"And the five million dollars?"

"Blown up, just like you saw on the news."

"I bet," she said, raising an eyebrow. "You were exonerated. Why haven't you come forward?"

"I've found I can be more useful as a ghost," I answered truthfully. "My heart was never really in it as a cop."

"I know what you mean," she said ruefully.

"Success not all it's cracked up to be?" It was my turn to raise an eyebrow, so I did.

"You can say that again. Some days reinventing myself sounds pretty good." She shook herself out of her thoughts. "But you helped Farnham, and you probably saved my life. You said you needed help, and I've got company coming soon."

Right. I told her about our effort to damage the flow of guns coming into the city, about our potential identification of the source, all without giving away too many details.

"Well," she said when I finished. "I'm impressed. You weren't kidding when you said you were trying to do more good as a ghost." She looked thoughtful. "I'm from that neighborhood, you know. Lawndale."

Diamond White

"Really?" I couldn't contain my surprise.

She looked down at her expensive clothes and laughed. "I know, right?" And then she looked sad. "You're doing more for my family than I am."

"Well, wanna help?"

"Of course. I'll call you the minute I find something."

"Actually, I'm trying to stay off the radar, but here is the number for my associate, Ms. Park." I threw her the piece of paper, which was wrapped around a bundle of bills.

"What's this?" she asked, confused. "You don't have to pay me."

"It's three thousand dollars," I said, looking at my feet. "I stole it from you when I was on the run."

She threw her head back and laughed, getting there quickly.

"You were busing tables at The Drake! I don't even remember what you looked like."

"No one ever does."

She shook her head. "You're an odd one, Riley. You give me back three thousand dollars, but you keep the five million."

"Yeah, about that." I opened the bedroom door, and we both walked back out to the kitchen. "I'm pretty sure it all blew up in the explosion at my apartment, but if it didn't, let's just say it's being used to make the city a better place."

"Listen," she said, "don't worry about it. It was worth four million dollars just to have Aldo Frances behind bars."

"And the other million?" I asked perplexed.

"That was just for watching you make Ferris Farnham look like the arrogant ass that he is, right in his own office." She grinned. "I can't thank you enough."

"My pleasure," I smiled.

16

The next day, I finally met Mrs. Right. She had a duplex on Roscoe, in the western part of the city. It was across the street from a Catholic school and a few doors down from Chopin Park, where I could run and work out.

She was an elderly lady who lived on the first floor with three cats, five thousand framed pictures of her grandchildren, and too much furniture. She was maybe seventy-five or eighty; ever since spending time with Uncle Elgort, I had been trying not to just think of anyone over seventy as "old." It was prejudicial, just throwing everyone into one big group, when they were as varied and deserving of individual attention as anyone else. I still don't like little kids, though. One step at a time.

As she served me tea, we sat in her impossibly old-fashioned living room, hemmed in on all sides by side tables, antique lamps, and easy chairs. On a stand in the corner was a 19" television, the old tube kind, that was as deep as it was tall and wide. I hadn't seen one of those in years.

"Many visitors, Miss McKay?" She asked, setting a china cup down next to me.

"Hmm?" I startled, distracted by all the bric-a-brac.

"I asked if you intend to have many visitors." She sat down opposite me, and instantly one of the cats, a black shorthaired one, was in her lap.

"Oh, no. Not me," I said shyly. "Well, maybe my cousin, Georgette once in a while, when she's visiting the city."

"Boyfriends?"

"I'm sorry?"

"I don't mean to pry, dear, it's just that my last tenants...they seemed so...normal when they first moved in. The young man had smart clothes and a crewcut. I thought perhaps he had been in the service. But..."

I leaned forward, like I was interested in hearing a juicy tale.

"Noise all hours. People coming and going. Motorcycles!" she said in a scandalized voice.

"Well," I said hastily. "I don't even have a car." Mental note: park Gromet down the street. "What happened to them?"

"They left in the middle of the night, owing six months' rent."

I gasped. "No!"

"Yes, they did. Just left all their belongings, furniture— if you could call it that—clothes, even. I've made an appointment with some movers next week to come and clear the whole place out."

I liked the neighborhood. It was residential, and no one would ever think to look for an international woman of mystery like myself there. I liked Mrs. Right. I was tired of hunting around. And I didn't have any furniture.

"I'll tell you what, Mrs. Right. I'll make you a deal: I'll pay you up front for six months, and you can just leave everything in the apartment. I'll get rid of anything I can't use. But, I get to move in right away, I need a place to live, starting tonight."

"Okay, my dear. It's a deal." She shooed the cat off her lap and stood up slowly. "Let me at least lend you some clean sheets."

"Thank you," I said, setting down the cup and saucer and rising to my feet. "And to answer your question, I do have a gentleman friend who may visit once in a while. But he's very well behaved, and he's going to love you; he's a fan of antiques."

She turned and looked at me with an alarmed expression.

Diamond White

"The furniture!" I said hastily. "I didn't mean you. He likes antique furniture."

The apartment was hilarious. First of all, their idea of "furniture" was a mattress on the floor, an old couch with one of the cushions missing, and a folding table and two folding chairs. For ambiance, there was a giant Fear City poster on one wall, an old eighties-style boom box on the floor, and for some reason the hardwood floor had been painted flat black. In the kitchen I found two plates, five pint glasses, and some mismatched silverware. The refrigerator was running, but I slammed it shut immediately after peeking in. That was going to be an all-day project.

I had more luck in the bedroom where, heaped on the floor, was a pile of his and hers black clothing. It didn't smell great, but there was a laundry in the basement. Even better, there were half a dozen pairs of leather boots, three of them in my size, including some really awesome Belleville combat boots. Yes, I had a million dollars buried in a steel suitcase in the backyard of Ruby's cottage, but scoring free boots is scoring free boots.

In the back of the closet I found two tool chests. One contained a well-maintained set of mechanics tools—our previous tenant was either an auto mechanic or hoped one day to be—and the other contained bolt cutters, a hack saw, a drill and other tools that I associated with disassembly, destruction, and perhaps theft of personal property.

I put the rose-patterned sheets that Mrs. Right had given me on the mattress, found my toothbrush and toothpaste in my satchel, and brushed.

It was early, but I climbed in bed anyway, lying back and staring at the ceiling, thinking of Nick. I had a breakfast meeting with Uncle Elgort in the morning, and I was hoping Nick would be there. I thought about my mixed feelings: I wanted to keep it cool and unattached, but at the same time I wanted more, always more, every time I was with him.

I held up my left hand in front of my face in the dim glow of the streetlight (there were no shades or curtains, of course). As always, I imagined my missing fingers, back where they belonged. In the distance, I heard the sound of a baseball game; they must be playing under the lights. I was once again visited by the knowledge that no one in the world knew where I was. It was bittersweet. When my hand got too heavy to hold up, I let it fall and closed my eyes.

17

The address I had for the breakfast meeting took me to a fancy Polish restaurant on Belmont. As I parked my bike and took off my helmet, I heard a wolf whistle, and looked quickly to my left. In front of the Progressive Truck Driving School, a man smoking a cigarette was leering at me. Nice. Guess the place wasn't actually as progressive as its name. Still, smoking and whistling at the same time, that's a talent that will land him a really excellent wife.

I ignored my new suitor and pushed on the door to the restaurant, even though the sign said, "Closed." I took off my coat and hung it on a hook in the foyer, stopping to straighten my long black wig in the mirror.

A small, older woman startled me, appearing at my side like a whisper, and I followed as she led me wordlessly into the main dining room. All the lights were out except at the back, where a long table was lit with an overhead chandelier.

Seated at the table were Uncle Elgort, Don, Nicky (with a smile and a raised eyebrow), Alden Earl, and two men I had never seen before. One I immediately pegged as a cop, just from his posture and expression. He was about forty-five with brown hair and a bit of a paunch. The other man looked to be in his twenties, possibly Latino. He was well dressed, but it looked uncomfortable on him, and I could see red irritation around his neck from shaving very recently. The table was immaculately set with a clean white tablecloth and linens.

Elgort rose as I approached, and I gave him a quick hug before taking an empty seat straight across from Nick.

"This is Georgette Wrigley," he said to the table, "an associate of mine, and a civil rights lawyer."

Diamond White

Captain Earl, sitting across from me next to Nick, gave me a quizzical look—he clearly recognized me from the other night—but said nothing about my name change from McKay to Wrigley.

"This," Elgort continued, indicating the middle-aged man, "is Al Hanson. He's with the Fourth District. He's heading up an anti-gun task force called GRAD—Gun Recovery and Disposal." Al gave me a curt nod.

"And this," said Elgort, with a gesture toward the younger man, "is Jorge Alvarez. He is one of the leaders of Latin Pride."

"Gay rights?" I asked. Alvarez immediately scowled at me.

"They're a street gang," growled Hanson, with obvious disdain. This attracted the attention of Alvarez, who swiveled his scowl toward the cop.

"A leader," Elgort pushed on, "who, like so many of us, has seen enough gun deaths in Chicago and wants to do something about it."

"Strange bedfellows," said Earl in his deep bass voice, directing his comment at Hanson. The cop leaned back, clearly cowed by the reputation of the great Captain Earl. "We're all here because we've agreed to explore unorthodox measures."

"And I'll remind you," said Don, speaking for the first time. "That we are all here under the expectation of complete confidentiality. This is strictly need-to-know."

The small woman from earlier came out of the kitchen, laden with steaming plates. Eggs, sausages, and some kind of blackberry porridge that looked fantastic. I removed my gloves and put them in my satchel, keeping my left hand under the table as I served myself some eggs and porridge.

102

Diamond White

Nick held out his plate, and I handed him the serving spoon. As the only woman at the table, I was not going to set the precedent of serving food. No way.

Don was going through what we knew about Jared Dexter and Antonio Negron.

"Negron is a bit of a cipher," he was saying, "but we are in the process of gathering information on him that we hope we will be able to put to use."

"What's the plan for Dexter?" asked Hanson. Alvarez kept quiet, but I noticed him keenly watching the others, especially the cops. He was at the table, but he was clearly reserving trust.

"Right. Dexter," said Uncle Elgort, and took a sip of coffee. Mmm, coffee. No sooner did I look around for the small woman then she was at my elbow, pouring fabulous smelling coffee from a small pot. The woman was a certified ninja. Polish Restaurant Ninja.

"The four of you," began Don, indicating Hanson, Earl, Alvarez, and myself, "have a 9 a.m. meeting tomorrow morning with Dexter to discuss the GRAD program. We booked it about four weeks ago. We also launched a website, and got a nice mention in the *Tribune* about a fundraiser we held in July."

Eldon Shelby, it seemed, loved the long con. You could see his eyes twinkling as he talked.

"Georgette volunteers her time pro bono to the organization. She's going to explain the program to him, in which Alvarez uses his influence with south side gangs to agree to an arms buyback. The police department, represented by Alden and Al, will explain that the Chicago PD will fund the buyback and dispose of the firearms. We want Dexter to help us with the PR, and to arrange some press opportunities with the mayor."

"I don't see what that gets us," said Alvarez bluntly.

"Just a lot of guns off the street," countered Hanson.

"But if he is who you say he is, he'll just sell more guns to the bangers."

"That," said Don with a grin, "is certainly what we hope he will do."

"I don't get it," said Hanson.

Earl laughed his deep, resonant laugh.

"What?" said Hanson, reddening.

"It's Uncle Elgort, Al," said Earl. "You're too young to remember those days. But trust me, with Uncle Elgort, there was always a play behind the play."

Uncle Elgort wasn't the blushing type, but he did nod his head lightly toward Earl in acknowledgement of the compliment.

"So what's the play?" asked Jorge Alvarez, looking at the old mob boss.

Uncle Elgort nodded toward Don.

Don leaned forward, elbows on the table, his fingers stitched together.

"Listen..."

18

"What do *you* think, Miss Wrigley?" asked Jared Dexter.

"What? Oh, yes, absolutely," I agreed. I had been distracted, staring at Nick's Degas sculpture, still sitting on the cadenza. Dexter had found the bug, but evidently hadn't realized that the statue itself had been swapped. Nice job, Nicky.

"Well, then," he said, rising. "I think we're done here. I look forward to working with you all on this very rewarding project." He came around his desk and shook hands with Hansen and Earl and myself. He hesitated a split second, then also shook hands with Alvarez.

Dexter was a short, slightly stocky man with boyish blond hair and a trim brown beard. He dressed very well in a black suit with nice wingtip shoes. I again looked around his office; I'd been a little preoccupied the last time I was here. Pictures with governors, senators, even a president. Plaques from neighborhood societies and state-wide charities. A set of golf clubs in one corner, looking mostly ceremonial. A bookshelf full of titles pertaining to politics and the law.

We had made our pitch for GRAD and now it was time for Act II. I opened the door with my right hand, keeping my left in my coat pocket.

"Thank you so much for your time, Mr. Dexter," I said.

"It was my pleasure, Ms. Wrigley" he answered, his eyes inadvertently sweeping down my suit. "Let me know if there is anything at all I can do for you."

Earl put his hand on my shoulder to steady himself, and we walked slowly out into the cubicle area. Over my shoulder I heard Al Hansen, still in Dexter's office, say, "Actually, Mr. Dexter—Jared—there's one more thing Jorge and I would like to discuss with you."

We left them behind, making our way to the elevator and down to the lobby, where we had to pass through the security checkpoint to leave the building. No sooner had we stepped onto the sidewalk then Don rolled up smoothly in the limousine. Captain Earl never had to wait for a ride, it seemed.

We climbed into the back, where Nick was already seated.

"How'd it go?" he asked.

"Pfft," I said, dismissively. "That was the easy part. It's up to Jorge and Al now."

"Quite the combo."

"Yes, I think they'll be taking their act on the road when all this is over. You should hear Al sing."

Earl gave his deep laugh.

"I don't think Al Hansen has ever sung, or even smiled, in his entire life. But," he sighed, "he's a good cop."

The second part of the meeting, the part without Earl and I, was where the trap would be laid. Jorge would lightly mention that he had a friend, Antonio Negron, who had mentioned to him that Dexter might be the kind of person willing to co-operate for mutual benefit. Since no one in the states supposedly knew much, if anything, of Negron, this would give Alvarez insider status. It's possible that Dexter would mention Alvarez to Negron, but that was a risk we had to take. I was hoping that Dexter would want to present the idea to Negron as his own.

Hansen would then explain that it would be his job to collect and destroy all the guns they bought from the citizenry of south Chicago. He had an idea, however, that perhaps instead of destroying the guns, Dexter might find a market for them in another part of the city. In a few months, when GRAD moved on to focus on other gangs, Alvarez would broker the repurchase of guns for Latin Pride, with a commission for himself.

Diamond White

The idea was Eldon's, based on what happened with bikes on campus. At Northwestern, locks were snipped with bolt cutters, bicycles were stolen, thrown into big trucks, and carted over to the University of Chicago. Sold cheap. While the trucks were there, locks were snipped, bicycles stolen, carted back to Northwestern, bought by kids who needed to replace their stolen bikes. Wait a week, and you could likely buy your original bike back on its return trip. And so the cycle went, for ever and ever, amen.

The whole scam with Dexter depended on Hansen being able to sell himself as a disgruntled cop, forced into this ridiculous charity as part of community service for some bad arrests. If a grouchy and mean-spirited demeanor were what it took to sell the act, then Hansen was home free. And then, hopefully, Dexter would give us information on Negron.

Alden and Elgort would arrange for Dexter to get caught with his hand in the cookie jar, and he would be arrested and publicly discredited. His days as an incognito arms dealer would be over. If Dexter named Hanson as an accomplice, Al would receive a slap on the wrist and an early retirement.

We dropped Earl off at his house. I helped him out of the car and walked him up to his front door.

"Thank you, Miss Wrigley," he smiled, "but I must say, I like you better as a redhead."

"But I'm smarter as a brunette," I told him.

"Hmm. Well, I'm sure there's quite a story there somewhere, but old Elgort's been keeping mum about you."

"Well, Uncle Elgort's a very smart man. Smart enough to make a deal with you. Can't have been easy."

Alden laughed. "Too true. But if it works? It's worth it. People change."

Diamond White

"I know I do."

"Yes, that's obvious. Goodbye, my dear, and be careful."

I skipped back down the stairs, and climbed in the back seat next to Nick, who looked out the window as Captain Earl entered his house and closed the door.

"Well," he said, "he likes you."

"I know, did you see us making out?"

"No, I must have missed that bit."

"Turns out he has a thing for redheads *and* for brunettes," I said, pulling off my black wig and ruffling my short hair with my hand.

"And why not," said Nick as the car pulled away. He reached into his jacket pocket and took out two small felt pouches, one black and one blue.

"Is that what I think it is?" I asked, my eyes widening.

"Kay..." Nick said in a stern voice.

"Nick..." I said back, fake serious.

"I need you to concentrate."

"But you're so cute, and my little girl brain just gets all confused when you're around."

Don snorted in the front seat. At least someone thought I was funny.

"Blue bag," Nick went on, ignoring me, "real diamonds."

"Blue, real. Worth how much, you think?"

"All together? Somewhere between $800,000 and a million and a half. It would depend on where and when you tried to sell them."

I gave a low whistle.

"Yes," he placed the bag in my good hand and curled my fingers shut over it. "Try not to lose it." Then he opened the black bag and poured the diamonds out into his hand.

"Black bag," he said, "fakes."

Diamond White

"Holy crap, Nicky," I gasped. "These are incredibly...incredible. What are they made of?"

The fakes shone dazzlingly bright in the late morning sun.

"Silicon carbide," he said. "Moissanite. It'll fool Salerno, and maybe Dexter, for a while. If this Negron is the big bad he's supposed to be, he'll probably have experts on hand who will know they're fake just by looking at the light refraction, but by that time it hopefully won't matter."

He put the diamonds back in the bag.

"You don't think she'll bring a diamond expert to your rendezvous, do you?"

"Rendezvous," I said, rolling the word around my tongue. "You make it sound so sexy." I took the black pouch from his hand and put it in my pocket. I moved a bit closer to him and put my good hand on his chest.

"It's not meant to be sexy," he said, exasperated.

"You only say that because you haven't met her," I purred in his ear.

"And I hope not to, after everything I've heard about her." He put his hand over mine and squeezed. "Be careful."

19

I struggled to get the baby jogger over the curb and into Millennium Park. New respect for moms, that's for sure. I looked around carefully. It was late afternoon, and the sun was sinking toward the Cultural Center. There were throngs of tourists. If we'd had our little motorcycle escapade on a day like this, we'd have probably killed some people.

I passed the big LED fountain, where kids were stomping through the water, even though it was a little chilly today, and headed over to the great lawn as people were gathering for the music festival. Way in the back I found a good bench and parked the jogger next to it, sitting down slowly and moving the long blond hair out of my face. I was wearing red plastic-rimmed glasses, a white tank top with a grey cardigan, and a flowery skirt that reached to my ankles.

I leaned into the stroller and carefully removed my bundle of joy. Well, bundle of blankets. I held it to my chest and slipped my left hand in among the bunched-up swaddling. This hid my missing fingers, but also gave me quick access to the container of mace hidden within.

Then I waited, and watched. And waited. After about fifteen minutes, a little girl marched up to me. She was probably seven, but was dressed like a hooker. A sparkly tank top, and shorts that said "Juicy" across the butt. I don't want to sound like my mother, but if she were my kid...

"Can I pet your baby?" she asked.

"No, sweetie. You can't, she's sleeping."

The girl rocked back and forth on her heels.

"What's her name?"

"Esmerelda, what's yours?"

"Kayleigh," she said. "With a Y and a GH."

Diamond White

I was trying to work out how that went together when her mother called her from the grass across the walkway. Kayleigh shrugged and turned away, almost run over by a herd of eight or ten young women jogging past in a group. Maybe a University team. One of them suddenly plopped down on the bench, panting.

"There you are," she said. "Do you have any water?"

Holy crap, it was Salerno, wearing a tight black tank top and black spandex running shorts, her long brown hair in a ponytail. She wore a brace on her left wrist.

"Damn, you're good," I said, reaching into the stroller with my free hand and handing her a bottle of water. "How'd you know it was me?"

She took a long drink of water, then shrugged. "I'm a professional, you know? It's what I do. Why'd you even bother with the disguise? The police think you are dead now, no?"

"I wanted to see you coming before you saw me coming, just to be safe."

Selena leaned back, her elbows on the back of the bench, the water bottle still in her left hand. Sweat glistened on her neck and chest. "I see your little chihuahua made a full recovery," she said, nodding across the field to where Ellery Park stood next to a lamp pole, watching us intently while pretending to be reading a Stella Wilkinson book. She was wearing a golf visor down low over her brow, a pink Izod shirt, yellow capris, and Birkenstocks.

"Great," I deadpanned, "you made my sidekick already. You nearly killed her, you know."

"Only nearly. You nearly broke my wrist, but only nearly." She took another drink, and then handed the bottle back to me. "And the loco Ukranian?"

"Czech."

Diamond White

"Whatever. I told you to come alone. Is she lurking around here, too?"

"Well, we'll just have to wait and find out." I tightened my grip on the mace. "Do you have something to trade with me?"

"In the office building, the other night, how did she make that explosion?"

I laughed and took a swig from the bottle.

"She put the magazine from her pistol in the toaster and started it up. It took a minute to get up to temperature."

Selena chuckled that low, sexy laugh of hers and shook her head.

"*Es loco, sí?*"

"Oh, she's crazy all right," I laughed along with her for a few seconds, then let it fade. "Now, to business. I don't like sitting out here with a million dollars in diamonds. Do you have the information?"

"That reminds me," said the young woman. "I forgot to bring your phone. Do you want it back?"

"No, you keep it. I may need to get in touch with you again."

"That Words with Friends game, on your phone. Do they make it *en Español?*"

"I don't know. Probably."

"It's addicting."

She reached behind her back and pulled a tiny thumb drive from her waistband. I reached my right hand into the swaddle of blankets and pulled out the pouch of diamonds, offered them in my outstretched palm. She picked up the pouch and dropped the thumb drive into my hand. She opened the pouch a tiny bit, just enough to let some light in, and then she pulled the drawstring shut again. She bowed her head for a moment and sighed a long sigh, said something under her breath in Spanish.

"*Gracias*, Red Riley," she said, standing up and tucking the pouch into the back of her shorts. "*Lo siento*."

I stood up, too.

"You're sorry?" I looked her in the eye. "There's nothing on this drive, is there?"

"Trust me, Riley, you do not want to go looking for trouble with Negron. He terrifies me. Me! He'd rip you into little pieces, just for fun. I wouldn't screw you over like this if my life weren't on the line."

"You talk like you're doing me a favor," I said in a steely voice. "But we aren't friends."

I whipped my left hand out to the side, sending the baby blanket flying. She followed it with her eyes, almost caught off guard as I swung the can of mace back in her direction and sprayed it.

Almost. She turned her head to the side, the spray hitting the back of her head, while grabbing my wrist expertly with her left hand. She yanked hard as she turned, pulling me with her and chopping the mace out of my hand with a strong blow from her free hand. The can hit the cement walkway and rolled under the bench.

I yanked backward, and she caught me off balance by leaping forward with me, thrusting her right leg forward, and hooking her foot behind my ankle while she continued to push forward. We both toppled onto the grass beside the path, rolling over twice before stopping with her body pressed full-length on top of me.

People must have been staring, but I couldn't see past Selena's head. Her cheek was pushed hard up against mine, so that we were looking past each other—she at the grass and me at the sky. Her strong arms were trapping mine against my sides. I struggled once, twice, but couldn't move. I could yell for help, but that wasn't the best move at the moment.

"Oh, *chica*," she purred into my ear. "I feel something has come between us."

"There's no us, you crazy—"

"I mean between our bodies, *chica*. I feel something hard between our bodies. Are you wearing a wire?"

"I'm just happy to see you," I grunted, trying to throw her off.

She snaked her right leg up to my elbow, holding my left arm to my side while her right hand slipped between us, pushing its way until it gripped the pouch that was hidden in my bra. She tried to pull it out, but realized it was inside my shirt.

"Get. Off." I spat as she ripped my shirt at the collar, reaching her hand down in until she could grab the drawstring and pull the pouch free.

"Eureka," she said, which I'm pretty sure isn't Spanish. "Not a wire. Diamonds. I guess you were right, Riley You really aren't my friend." She leapt to her feet in one smooth motion. I sat up slowly, non-threateningly. "This little trick of yours would have been my death sentence with Negron. If I hadn't felt that bump, I wouldn't even have considered you would double cross me. I guess I think too highly of you. Well, I won't make that mistake again."

"If Negron is so evil," I said, "don't give it back to him. Hide. Let me help you!"

With a sad look on her face, she reached back and pulled out the black pouch, tossing it into my lap. She tucked the blue pouch back where the blue one had been.

"It doesn't work that way," she said, stepping off the grass and back onto the path. "*Adios, chica.*"

And she was gone.

Diamond White

Moments later Park was pulling me to my feet.

"Now you show up," I said with exasperation.

"You said observe, not interact!" She looked at me shrewdly. "Were you two making out on the ground behind the bench?"

"Hardly," I said wryly.

"Because that's what it looked like. Just sayin'."

I brushed myself off, watching Selena's tiny figure jogging off in the far distance.

"What's wrong?" asked Park, noticing my long face. "Didn't your plan work?"

"It did," I said, picking up the blanket and tossing it in the stroller. "And now I feel kind of bad about it." I looked down at the pouch in my hand, gave it a squeeze, and put it in the pocket of my cardigan. They were the real diamonds. Selena had the fake ones.

Had I really just signed her death warrant?

20

"I'm sorry, Kay," said Uncle Elgort, seated uncomfortably in the easy chair. "I didn't realize how bad things had gotten."

We were sitting in my mom's room at Honeywell. She was sitting on the side of her bed, staring out the window. Nick stood by the bookshelf, perusing the titles. I sat next to Mom on the bed, brushing her long auburn hair. She paid no attention to any of us.

"The Christmas cards coming every year," Elgort went on. "I assumed she was more cognizant."

"She had help sending them," I said, glumly. The good news, of course, was that Mom hadn't been distraught by the announcement of my death on the evening news. The bad news, of course, was that she hadn't much noticed when I came by to tell her I was still alive.

Nick pulled out a copy of *Blood Meridian* and was examining it carefully.

"I suppose it's for the best," I sighed. "There's no one now. Apart from Marty and Ruby, and they are well aware of the risks."

Nick looked up from the book. Raised an eyebrow at me.

"Well, yes. The Shelbys. But I'm pretty sure you lot can look after yourselves. Mom would have been happy, I think, to know that we've reconnected. She was always more copacetic about it than Dad."

"Your father was a police officer, Kay. And we were criminals. You couldn't expect him to be pleased with his brother's choice of profession."

I turned and looked at Uncle Elgort.

"*Were* criminals?"

"Well," he coughed. "I suppose yes, we are still criminals in a way."

"In many, many ways," said Nick.

117

Diamond White

"True. But no more of the violence. No more bending others to our will. Now we just look for the mistakes of others, and exploit them for our benefit."

"And," I chimed in, "your targets are certainly not innocent."

"For the most part," said Nick, with a dour expression.

"Well, certainly Dexter," I argued.

"Without a doubt, Dexter," said Elgort.

"I'm sorry I wasn't able to get any more information on Negron," I sighed.

"Not yet, my dear. Not yet. There will be other chances."

"And Dexter?" I asked.

"He seems very interested in our little proposition, the recycling of the guns. He told Hansen that he needed to talk with his people."

"Negron?"

"I assume so, but perhaps the mayor himself. Who knows where this will lead. We shall see. In the meantime, your job is to find Selena Salerno without her finding you, and continue to push for information about Antonio Negron."

"Simple," I said lightly, standing up and clapping my hands. Mom flinched, and I hurried to rub my hand on her shoulder, put her at ease. "I've always wanted to go to Mexico."

Nick turned around sharply, wanting to interrupt, but not wanting to tell me what to do. Elgort showed no such restraint.

"Under no circumstances are you to go anywhere near Negron, Kay. Do you understand?"

I didn't like to be given orders, but I also remembered the look of fear on Selena's face when she spoke of Negron. She was the biggest bad-ass I'd ever met, and she was terrified.

Diamond White

"I understand," I said, taking Uncle Elgort's hand and helping him out of the chair.

"This book is worth some good money," said Nick, holding up the copy of *Blood Meridian*.

"I'll keep that in mind after I've spent all the diamonds," I replied.

He grimaced at me and put the book back on the shelf.

"Kidding!" I said, and held my hands out to each side, palms up in supplication.

Unexpectedly, Mom reached out and grabbed my left hand in both of hers. She pulled it close to her face, and ran her index finger along the hard, pink scar tissue.

"Missing," she said quietly.

"I know, Mom."

"Ouchie," she said.

"No kidding, Mom. No kidding."

21

Later, just after 1 a.m., something went bump in the night. Nick woke with a start, rolled over and fell out of bed. Since my bed is currently just a mattress on the floor, it wasn't much of a drop, and didn't make much noise.

In the dim light, he fumbled for his clothes on the floor, listening intently. Another slight noise, coming from the living room. He pulled on a t-shirt that was lying on the floor, and was pulling on a pair of pants when the door of the bedroom opened, a flashlight beam catching him in the face, then panning down to where he was fumbling with his pants.

"Don't you wear underwear?" asked a skeptical woman's voice. Two shadowy figures had entered the room.

"Can't find them," said Nick, remaining unflappable as always, "in this glare. Could you please?"

"No, we don't please," said a man's voice, and the flashlight moved closer to Nick, who took a step back until he was against the wall.

"Kay?" said Nick tentatively.

"No, it's not okay," said the man, his voice was young and angry, perhaps a bit intoxicated. "It's not okay at all. There's something here we need, and we're going to take it. You stay out of our way, you don't get hurt. *Okay*?"

"It's not me I'm worried is going to get hurt," said Nick, with bravado.

The intruder laughed. Probably sneered, too, but it was dark.

"Did you here that, lover? He's going to hurt me!!"

There was silence.

"Sherry?"

He turned and swept the room with the flashlight, but Sherry was nowhere to be seen. The room was empty.

Diamond White

Out in the living room, Sherry couldn't speak because my right hand was covering her mouth while my left was squeezing her throat tightly. I had yanked her soundlessly out of the bedroom doorway and now had her pushed up against the adjoining wall. She tried to stomp on my foot, but I evaded her shoe and squeezed harder on her windpipe until she stopped.

Light spilled from the doorway as the flashlight swept past, then returned as the intruder stepped through the door and back into the living room, turning to shine the light all the way around the space.

"Sher?"

Just as the light reached us I let go of Sherry and ducked, driving my left fist into Sherry's stomach while kicking out hard to the side with my right foot, catching her sweetie's leg on the side, just above the knee. It didn't break the leg, but it was a good hit, and he went down hard, the flashlight briefly illuminating the ceiling before spinning wildly around as he hit the ground.

Sherry, was also on the ground, the wind knocked out of her, her knees pulled up to her chest and a keening sound coming from her mouth. I stood back up as Nick came out of the bedroom. He reached over and flicked on the overhead light.

The intruders were a young man and woman, both skinny and dressed in black. Both with heads shaved and many piercings. The man was holding his leg with one hand, with the other he reached for the heavy flashlight next to him on the floor.

"Touch it," I warned him, "and I break all your fingers."

He pulled his hand back in.

"They don't look like diamond thieves," said Nick.

"I don't think they are," I said. Nick was looking at me strangely. "What?"

"You're wearing my boxer shorts."

Diamond White

"Well, I was in a hurry," I snapped back.

They just wanted their tools, and their boots. And maybe, ma'am, if it wasn't too much trouble, that poster on the wall?

Nick took down the poster and rolled it up while I looked through their wallets and their cell phones. I wrote down their names and numbers. James, the man, sat at the table holding a bag of ice to the side of his leg, his knee was swelling up already. Sherry had gotten her breath back, and was sitting on one of my unpacked cardboard boxes, watching me glumly.

I stood with my hands on my hips, giving them my old tough cop stare.

"...you could have gotten yourselves killed, not to mention you could have woken up Mrs. Right," I droned on. James was staring intently, I thought at my midriff, which was showing between my sports bra and my boxers. Then I realized he was staring at my damaged hand. I pointed at him with my two good fingers.

"Pay attention when I'm talking to you."

"Do you really have diamonds?" Sherry asked.

"No, of course I don't. Would I be living here if I did?"

"So are you calling the cops, or what?" asked James, ready for this ordeal to be over.

"No, though I should. Take your crap and get out of here."

A few minutes later they were treading as softly as possible down the stairs and out to their incredibly unsafe looking Honda Accord, which was at least as old as they were. They got the tools in the trunk, then came back for the boots and the poster. Sherry was put out when she found out I was keeping the pair of Belleville combat boots, but really, how many pairs of boots did she need?

Diamond White

I closed the door on them and sighed, then started to chuckle. I turned around to see Nick coming out of the kitchen, a glass of water in his hand. He started to laugh, too.

"I thought they'd never leave," he said.

"I'm hungry," I said. "I don't know if I can get back to sleep."

He set the glass on the table and walked over to me.

"I'm hungry, too," he said, slyly. "And I definitely don't want to go back to sleep."

"Really, what did you have in mind?"

"Well first," he said with a grin, reaching out and grabbing my waistband, "I want my boxer shorts back."

22

I walked into the reception area of Technology Acquired and was met by an unfamiliar face. And a really big neck. And huge shoulders. The guy was massive, shoe-horned behind the reception desk. I didn't know they made collars big enough, but his shirt was buttoned all the way up and he even wore a tie.

I was wearing a mid-length blonde wig, motorcycle leathers, and my leather gloves. In one hand I carried my bright red helmet, in the other a brown paper bag with chocolate chip cookies from Roeser's Bakery.

The mountain began to rise behind the desk, but I motioned him back down, waving the paper bag in the air.

"Cook County medical courier," I said. "I'm here to collect a urine sample from Mr. Martynek."

The man grimaced at me.

"Red!" called Marty through the open door to his office. "Get in here, would you?"

I winked at Mountain Man and sashayed through the door, my leather pants and jacket squeaking as I did.

"I'm not Red today," I said, tossing the bag of cookies to him.

"Okay, Blondie," said Marty, his black hair falling into his eyes as he peered down into the bag. "My favorite!" he exclaimed with delight, withdrawing one of the cookies and taking a giant bite.

He waved me to a chair on the other side of his desk, but I instead reclined on the architecturally stunning, cantilevered sofa. It wasn't actually that comfortable.

He chewed a few more times and then swallowed, sitting behind his desk.

"Make yourself at home," he said, and started tapping on his keyboard.

"I was up half the night," I said, yawning.

Diamond White

"Oh? Do tell..."

"Not that. Well," I admitted, "a little bit of that."

"Speaking of which," he said, looking over at me, "tell me more about this Officer Park that I sort of met the other day."

"Eeew. No, that's not happening."

"Why not?" he asked indignantly. "You get to have midnight trysts, but I don't?"

"It's not that."

"Which one of us are you ashamed of?"

I closed my eyes and exhaled.

"Neither. I just want to keep things simple, and I'm sure that would be anything but simple."

"So I can't pursue her because it would inconvenience you?"

I sat up, with great effort. I was exhausted, and the sofa seemed designed to defeat me.

"Actually, yes. No." I pressed on when he opened his mouth to object. "Listen, I'm dead. No social network, no college buddies, no friends from work. In time, I can make new friends as Riley McKay, but frankly I haven't had any time. I just have you, and Ruby. Park, maybe. I'm trying not to get attached."

"And your new friend, the artist?"

"Nick."

"Are you ever going to introduce me to Nick? Even Auntie hasn't met him."

"I know. I'm trying to stay compartmentalized. There are some things it's better, safer that you don't know. I think Selena proved that. Is there any saving the bunker?"

He waved my concerns away with one hand, took another cookie with the other.

"It'll be okay. They'll gut it and rebuild it. It will be better, because I've suggested some security upgrades."

126

"Like Tristan out there?" I asked, motioning toward reception.

"Tristan? His name is Mike."

"Sure, okay, but wouldn't Tristan have been a better name, ironic?"

"Whatever." He made a few more clicks on his keyboard. "Come over here, I've got some stuff about your girlfriend."

I looked at him nonplussed.

"Salerno. Or, Selena as you call her."

"Yeah, not my girlfriend."

"Huh. Ellery said she saw you two getting it on in Millennium Park."

I walked behind his chair and put my hands, semi-playfully, around his throat.

"Ellery? Ellery? I thought you wanted me to introduce you?"

"Oh no," he said, shaking me off. "I introduced myself. I just wanted to know what you thought of her."

"No comment."

I reached over his shoulder and grabbed a cookie from the bag.

"Do you think Tristan could get us some milk?"

"That's not what Mike is there for."

"Speaking of Salerno," I segued, "show me what you've got."

Marty brought up a window that said "Audacity" at the top. In the frame was a graph of peaks and valleys: a sound file.

"I collected all the sound files from the bug in your old phone and had one of my techs scan through them for useful conversations." He turned to look at me. "Let me just say that your beautiful friend is definitely the strong, silent type. Four days of surveillance, and there's maybe an hour, total, of speech, and about a third of that is with you.

"There's a good amount of grunting and panting, which I really, really hope is her working out."

"Marty!"

"And then there's this." He reached forward and hit a key, and the little graph started to jump and dance as Selena's low, distinctive voice came from the small speakers.

"It's in Spanish."

"I know," said Marty, "but I used Google to translate it." He picked up a piece of paper and handed it to me. I read it aloud.

The meeting did not go as planned. I was unable to reconvene the diamonds.

"I think that's supposed to be recover," said Marty.

"Yeah, I get it."

"The auto translator isn't great. You'd think in this day and age—"

"Shush." I read on.

But I can get them.

You say you delivered them to dexterous, but they are not there. You say you get them back, but you doughnut. Why should I believe you?

Because I know the stakes.

You have ten days. When I arrive in shit cargo, I expect them in my hand.

You are coming to chick ago?

Friday. Do not this anoint me.

"Holy crap!" I exclaimed, looking up at Marty. "Negron is coming to Chicago!"

"Or Shit Cargo," laughed Marty. "Maybe we have nothing to worry about. Who's Negron?"

I filled Marty in. I had wanted to keep him out of it, but I felt bad about destroying the bunker, and his sudden need for heightened security. And like I said, I didn't have that many friends to share with. And a burden shared is... something. I can't remember. Better.

"I've never heard of Antonio Negron," said Marty when I had finished. "Not that I'm up on my Mexican crime lords. But if Salerno is afraid of him..."

"Exactly."

"She's going to be after you."

"And you. And Ruby. And Park."

"Shit."

"You need a dozen more Tristans out there."

"It's not me I'm worried about. She's not getting in here. Not even through the ductwork," he said, reading my mind. We both couldn't help but glance at the ceiling. "It's Auntie I'm worried about. And Ellery. Maybe I should invite Ms. Park to stay with me for a while."

I rolled my eyes and picked up my helmet from the sofa.

"For safety!" he called after me.

I raised one leather-clad middle finger over my shoulder as I headed for the door.

23

Over the course of the next week, someone tried to break into Technology Acquired twice. Presumably it was Salerno, though she managed to avoid being caught on camera. Marty had all kinds of little sensors around the place, some of which included punitive responses like pepper spray, or electrified doorknobs.

We sent Ellery Park out of town, three days at Harry Potter World in Florida. I'm serious, that's where she wanted to go. Expecto geeko.

Ruby and I spent the time up at the lake, enjoying the last of the warm weather. The nights were getting cool, and the leaves were changing. I did a lot of kayaking, running, rock climbing. At night, Ruby taught me chess, but it was taking me some time to get it. You really have to learn to think several moves ahead. I'm pretty sure Ruby was trying to tell me something.

On Thursday, I borrowed Ruby's car and scoured antique shops and yard sales, picking up this and that for my apartment. I stopped at Wrightwood Furniture and bought several things to be delivered later that day.

On my way back to my place on Roscoe, I drove past Ruby's house in Wicker Park. I was tempted to stop and water her plants, but I was afraid of meeting an unwanted acquaintance. There weren't many entry points for Salerno, but Ruby's house was one of them. Since Park's little trick, Ruby had changed the title on the cabin, but her house in the city was still in her name. Like Park, Selena could figure out Ruby's name easily enough, and from there her address.

I was wise to be cautious, because during my drive-by I spotted a black BMW with someone sitting in the driver's seat. It's a good thing I wasn't on Gromet, or she would have made me easily. I passed by nonchalantly, turning at the first cross street, then doing a three-point

Diamond White

U-turn to head back for another look. Just as I turned back onto Ruby's street, Salerno hopped out of her car and jogged around to the back of Ruby's house. I pulled up next to the BMW and rolled down my window. Grabbing some napkins and a pen from the glove box, I wrote her a little note and tossed it through the open window onto the passenger's seat.

I was about to take off when I heard a strange thumping coming from the back of her car. I paused, listening. There it was again. By God, she had someone in the trunk! I was about to step out of the car when instinct grabbed me by the ear and turned my head toward Ruby's house. Selena Salerno was racing across the grass toward me!

I threw the Subaru in drive and stomped on the gas. The station wagon surged sluggishly forward, not the peppiest vehicle on the streets, but I started to pick up speed. Selena adjusted her trajectory across the yard and hit the street about five feet behind me.

"C'mon!" I shouted at the dashboard, stamping my foot all the way down to the floor as I approached a four-way stop. "Damn!"

I slowed just enough to make sure no one was coming, but it was all the opportunity Salerno needed. As I careened left around the corner, I heard a thump. I looked back to see her hanging from the luggage rack, scrambling to get her feet up on to the bumper.

Holy crap! I swerved left at the next intersection, trying to shake her off, but it was impossible to get up any speed in this neighborhood. She leaned out around the back quarter panel of the car, one hand holding the luggage rack, the other reaching for the rear side door. I turned into a back alley off LeMoyne and moved perilously close the brick wall of a building, trying to scare her off, but she had pulled herself up onto the top

Diamond White

of the car. There was a horrible metallic crunching sound as the passenger side of the Subaru collided with cement. Sorry, Ruby.

Up ahead the alley ended, the wall of an apartment building fast approaching. Damn.

Unwilling to slow down, I turned hard right at the end of the building on my right, keeping the wheel racked around and making a u-turn over the sidewalk and into a green courtyard on the back side of the row of buildings I'd just sideswiped. Nobody seemed to be out and about, which was a relief as I ran over someone's little plastic toddler car. I hope they had insurance.

I drove even faster until I could see an opening at the end of the courtyard. At the last instant, I slammed on the brakes and pulled hard to the left, skittering across the sidewalk and coming to a screeching halt, back on LeMoyne.

That did it. The g-forces were too much for Salerno and she flew off the roof of the Subaru. Narrowly missing the trunk of a tree on the far sidewalk, she landed on a grassy lawn, rolling over and over again until she came to a rest about twenty feet in.

I didn't have time to see if she was all right, as I was sitting stalled in oncoming traffic. A big, dark green Honda SUV came to a stop in a controlled skid, our grills almost touching. I waved my half hand at the ponytailed woman in the driver's seat and threw the wagon into reverse, backing up along the rest of the block until I could turn around and head off, my hands shaking on the wheel.

I woke up the next morning feeling great. My apartment looked more and more like a place in which someone might actually live. All the furniture I bought was from the clearance section. Mismatched and eclectic. It made it look like I had lived there forever.

Diamond White

Then I remembered not only my run in with Selena, but the damage to Ruby's car. Sure, we both had plenty of money, but she loved that old thing. I was never going to hear the end of it.

I stretched and did some calisthenics in the living room, which I had purposely kept sparse for this reason. I got dressed in running attire and went out and ran around the ball fields a few times. I'll admit it—I hate jogging. Yes, I'm becoming a fitness nut, but I just don't get the concept of running when you aren't being chased. Oh well.

An hour later I was showered and shaved when the doorbell rang twice, then I heard the door unlock at the bottom of the stairs. That had to be Nick. I looked in the mirror and thought about meeting him naked, but we didn't really have time for that this morning. I threw on red panties and a matching red bra, and pulled on a red sundress with small white polka dots. Summer wasn't going to last forever. I grabbed my climbing clothes and something less dressy to wear later in the day, and threw them in my satchel.

I found Nick in the kitchen/dining room, looking over the new dining room table and mismatched chairs with amusement. He was wearing faded jeans and a paint-stained white oxford shirt. Old leather shoes with no socks. When he turned and saw me his eyes lit up and he mouthed a silent, "Wow."

"Am I overdressed?" I asked, suddenly self-conscious.

"No, not at all. You look fantastic." He looked down at his own clothes. "I came straight from the studio, and I won't be at the meeting, so I didn't bother to change."

"You won't be there?" I said with an inadvertent pout.

"No, this is Don's show, and trust me, it's going to be a great show. My part is pretty small and I already know what to do." He looked past me at the tall standing lamp

134

in the corner, with the blue tasseled shade. "You bought furniture."

"Yes," I said, excited. "Isn't it great?"

"Well, it's distinctive." He looked back at me. "You know we sell furniture, right? At Shelby Furniture. It's not just a front. We actually sell the stuff. We could have given you a good discount."

I gave him a big hug, then stepped back.

"No offense, but I wanted something a little livelier. When we get married and buy a McMansion in Gurnee, then we can buy all the Shelby furniture you want."

He colored, embarrassed by the suggestion, which immediately made me color, too. Between the red dress and the hair and the blush, I'm sure I looked like a big red idiot.

"Not that we're getting married any time soon," I added, haphazardly.

"You haven't asked me yet," said Nick, recovering.

"I've been busy." I went to my new coatrack and took down a light black windbreaker and my satchel.

"Gurnee, huh?"

"Actually," I said, heading for the door, "I've been thinking a lot about the island of Vieques, when I get tired of playing Batwoman."

"I didn't know there was a Batwoman."

"I've upgraded Batgirl."

"Vieques?"

"Yeah, though I burn easily. How would you feel about painting in the tropics?"

"It worked for Gaugin," Nick said gamely, closing the door behind him.

24

I was leaning against the wall of the dealership, thumbing through news reports on my phone while waiting for Ruby to return from her test drive. Four different salesmen of various age and weight asked if they could assist me. A female salesperson sailed right by without a moment's hesitation.

I didn't look like much of prospect, I admit. Ruby had picked me up from the climbing wall and we had come straight into the city. I was wearing camouflage surplus pants and a black tank top, and my hands still had some white chalk on them.

Since leaving Kay Riley for dead, I hadn't paid that much attention to the news. I'd been in a constant zone of self-improvement, and I liked what it was doing for me. I was fitter, calmer, hopefully smarter. I had it in my mind that I was going to change the world for the better. Or at least Chicago.

So it was with disgust that I read about the eleven homicides in Chicago over the weekend. More than fifty people wounded in shootings. What the hell was wrong with the world? What the hell was wrong with people like Jared Dexter, making money and political gain off the deaths of our young people?

Elgort Shelby had a lot to answer for in his life, that's for sure. At least now he was trying to do something about it.

Unlike Elgort, if my life were a ledger, there'd be almost nothing on the bad side. However, there would be precious little on the good side either. Sure, I protected and served for ten years. Probably did a little bit of good here and there, but I couldn't help but think of all the opportunities I likely let pass. I wasn't a very good cop. Not particularly eager to go the extra mile.

Diamond White

We must each contribute according to our abilities, said...somebody. Well, my abilities were growing stronger by the day, and I intended to contribute.

I straightened my shoulders and slipped my phone in my pocket. When I looked up I saw a young man with an ill-fitting suit and an ill-advised mustache approaching.

"Hello," he said. "Are you car shopping, today Miss...?"

"Aguilera," I said, looking at him over my sunglasses. "I was actually looking for the motorcycle department."

"I'm, sorry, Miss Aguilera, we don't sell motorcycles here."

"You don't!" I leaned back against the wall and stuck out my lower lip. "But I had my heart set on trying one out."

I never found out his follow-up move, because a bright red Subaru wagon came tearing around the corner and screeched to a halt. The guy jumped a foot, and another, older salesman came striding quickly from his office, an aggravated look on his face.

"Ma'am," he began, as Ruby climbed out of the driver's seat and slammed the door. "I must insist that—"

"I'll take it," announced Ruby, cutting him off. "G.I Jane there will pay you."

"Oh. Well..." said the older man, adjusting his attitude.

"Are you sure, Ruby?" I asked. "I think you should get the Mercedes."

"Why" she asked, limping around the car toward me. "This is more practical, no?"

"Yeah, sure, but when they make a movie about my life I bet Mercedes will pay way more for product placement than Subaru will."

Papa Car Dealer looked at the two of us like we were crazy, but Sonny Car Dealer turned his attention back to me, his eyes again wandering down my body.

Diamond White

"But that is nonsensical," exclaimed Ruby with her rough accent. "When they make the movie, they can use whatever model car they want, right?"

"If they care nothing about verisimilitude, sure," I countered. "It's just, this is the same exact wagon, Ruby."

"No it isn't," she said indignantly, "it's a 2017 model. Havel was a 1998. Plus, it's red. Havel was green."

"Right," I said, admitting defeat. "You're absolutely right."

I turned to Sonny Car Dealer.

"How much will your dad give us for Havel?"

"He's *not* my dad," the guy said, indignantly.

"I'm sorry," Papa broke in. "Havel?"

"The old car," I explained. "Its name is Havel." I tilted my head toward Ruby and rolled my eyes to the men to indicate that she was perhaps mentally challenged.

"Well," he said, "I'm afraid that car has sustained quite a bit of damage to the body."

"Yeah, but you heard Ruby, it's an antique, right?"

"Not exactly..."

"And, we're paying cash," I added, pulling a wad of money from my pocket with my right hand.

The older man turned to his not-son. "Why don't you take this young lady inside and begin filling out the paperwork? I'll take another look at Mrs. Martynek's trade-in and see what we can do."

"So, Sonny," I said as we walked toward the showroom door.

"Seth," he interrupted.

"So, Seth," I continued as he held the door for me, "tell me about yourself."

25

I watched through binoculars as Jared Dexter entered the building of his very expensive acupuncturist in Lincoln Park, Nick entering right behind him.

I thumbed my walkie-talkie. "He's on his way in."

"Roger," answered Park. "Going quiet now."

"Good luck."

I crossed Wells St. and entered the building, wearing a blonde wig and nurse's scrubs, a bag of leftover Thai lunch in my hand. The glasses I wore were so thick I almost tripped up the stairs on my way in.

The reception area was elegant, if antiseptic. Dexter sat in a chair, looking at his phone. He had obviously been in a fight, or a car accident, very recently. His face was bruised, and there was gauze covering his left earlobe, red showing through. Nick sat in another chair reading *Golf Digest*. Behind the reception desk sat Margaret, Nick and Don's cousin, or maybe aunt—I could never quite get it right.

I wondered briefly who was selling furniture today at Shelby's, and smiled at the mental image of Uncle Elgort showing a young couple a living room set. Actually, he'd probably be pretty good at it.

"Back from lunch," I said breezily as I passed by reception and made my way to the back. I walked into an open treatment room, set down my leftovers, and pulled the syringe out of my scrubs pocket. I set it on the counter, then crossed the hall to peek into the other room.

The acupuncturist and his receptionist were both seated on office chairs, their hands tied behind their backs, duct tape over their mouths. Standing next to them was Park, wearing a gorilla mask and holding a gun. I could see from the doorway that there was no magazine in the weapon.

Diamond White

I approved of the sentiment and the safety of leaving it empty, but I also wanted to be sure Park was equipped to handle herself. She had returned from Orlando with a nasty black eye, and hadn't yet told Ruby or I what had happened. I looked back at the acupuncturist, who was a balding man in his sixties, and the receptionist who clearly spent too much time sitting at reception. El was in no immediate danger from those two.

I gave her the thumbs up, and she gave me a thumb's up back.

I returned to my room, picked up the syringe in my left hand, and covered it with a towel. This had the bonus of covering my disfigured hand. Didn't want Dexter to make the connection if he ever saw Georgette's hand.

I stuck my head into reception.

"Mr. Dexter," I said in a deep, throaty voice, "the doctor is ready for you."

He looked up at me in surprise. I don't think he had really noticed my earlier entrance, entranced by his phone as he was.

"Helene is out today, too?"

"Yep," said Margaret, before I could even respond. "She and Sylvie both had a bad lunch at the Whole Foods. Food poisoning. You got the B team today, I'm afraid."

Dexter stood and put his phone in his pocket. He chuckled good-naturedly.

"I'm sure you ladies will do just fine."

"I'm sure we will," I said and, as he walked past me, I dropped the towel and stuck the needle through his shirt and into the fleshy part of the back of his upper arm.

"Hey!" he bellowed. He slapped at his arm as if he'd been stung, grabbing the syringe and yanking it out. I turned my face away, because I didn't want him to recognize me. He seized my arm in anger, beginning to

142

pull me around toward him, but he wasn't as strong as me. He tried to cry out, but the only people in earshot were on the Shelby payroll. Finally, after a long minute, his grip loosened as the drug made its way into his bloodstream. A moment later he was on the floor, unconscious.

Park peeked her gorilla head out the door questioningly.

"All good," I told her, as Nick entered the hallway and bent down to check Dexter's pulse.

"Jesus," said Nick, "who tuned him up? Negron?"

"I don't think so," I said. I had a feeling I knew who had done it.

In the reception area, the front door opened and Don entered carrying a stretcher. Through the open door I could see an ambulance at the curb, lights flashing.

"Subtle," I said.

He rolled his eyes at me, and then he and Nick rolled Dexter onto the stretcher, lifted together in synchronization, and walked Dexter out to the curb. The first part of Don's plan had gone like clockwork.

"I almost feel bad for the guy," said Margaret. "First someone beats the crap out of him, now this."

"Yeah," I grinned. "Really tragic."

26

"Hello?"

"Good morning, Mr. Mayor. My name is Georgette Wrigley, I'm a civil rights attorney here in Chicago."

Panting breath. I'd caught him on his morning run.

"How do you have this number, Miss Wrigley? It's private."

"Is it? Well I had no idea. I'm so sorry, Mr. Dexter gave it to me some time ago."

"Jared?"

"Exactly, and that's why I'm calling you," I pressed on before he could get too sidetracked on how I might have acquired his cell phone number. "I work with Mr. Dexter on the GRAD program, buying back guns to lowe—"

"Yes, I'm familiar," he said curtly. He clearly didn't like his morning run interrupted. It was probably the only peace and quiet he got all day.

"Well I've discovered some serious irregularities. Guns missing, or not being destroyed. New guns flooding in."

"Well, that does sound like a problem, but I'm afraid I must refer you to Mr. Dexter on this matter."

"That's the problem," I told him, anxiety in my voice. "Nobody can find Mr. Dexter."

"What? What are you talking about."

"Mr. Dexter is missing," I said urgently. "Nobody at his office knows where he is. You don't think he had something to do with this, do you?"

"Wow, ah, I'm going to have to let you go, Miss—"

"Wrigley, like the field."

"Miss Wrigley, so I can look into this immediately. I will be in touch when I know more."

He clicked off.

Half an hour later the phone rang. A number I didn't recognize, and who has my number these days? I answered, figuring it was the mayor.

145

Diamond White

"Hello?"

"I need those diamonds," hissed Selena Salerno.

I held the phone between my ear and shoulder, which used to be so much easier with a landline; iPhones are slippery. I was in my kitchen putting together a salad and smoothies for my lunch guests.

"Selena! You've changed phones!" I said cheerily.

"Yes, the one you gave me, it had some issues."

"Well, that's too bad, it always worked well for me."

"You've got to stop messing in this game, *chica*. You are making your life in danger, and mine, too."

I reached into my new refrigerator, which I bought to replace the HAZMAT zone the previous tenants had left behind, and brought out some hummus and cherry tomatoes.

"You have to trust me, Selena, and not get in my way."

"Me?" she almost shouted, incredulous. "In your way! *Mierda*!"

"That visit you paid our friend Mr. Dexter, what was the point?"

She growled on the other end, or what sounded like growling. Sometimes when I picture Selena in my head, what I actually see is a spotted leopard, pacing back and forth, ready to leap on something.

"I was angry," she admitted. "He blamed the lost diamonds on me, brought some tough guys along to 'encourage' me to recover the diamonds more quickly. As if you-know-who isn't incentive enough."

"Voldemort?" I asked

"*Que*?"

"You said 'You-Know-Who,' as if Negron is He Who Must Not Be Named. You don't have Harry Potter in Chile?"

"The boy wizard, with the scar? *Claro*, of course."

"That's what I meant."

146

Diamond White

"I'm lost," said Salerno. "What were we talking about?"

"Dexter sent some men to incentivize you. That must have gone poorly."

"For them, *si.*" For the first time in the conversation, I heard the playful smile in her voice.

"Selena, please, stay out of the way. I've got a plan, and it's going to take care of your problem as well as mine."

She snorted. "I know I underestimated you before, Red, but really, what can you do against Negron?"

"That's where we are different," I told her. "You're a lone wolf, and I respect that. In fact, I'm having trouble with attachments getting in the way."

"You'd be surprised how much I understand that."

"Yes, well. Lone wolf is great, but sometimes you need friends."

"I just need the diamonds," she said, the humor gone from her voice.

She hung up.

"Okay," I said, brightly, carrying the tray with the smoothies and the salad into the dining room. "Sorry for the delay. Old friend, important business."

They both looked at me when I entered. Sherry was in the middle of the room, standing staring at the giant framed Jackson Pollock print on the long wall. She seemed transfixed.

She was wearing black leather boots and black jeans with rips all over them. A big black leather belt with a silver buckle, a form fitting tank top that only partially covered a black lace bra. Madonna, from a phase before Sherry was even born. Hell, does the world just keep repeating itself over and over and over?

"Did you do this?" she asked, pointing at the print.

"No, it's a Jackson Pollock. It's at the Art Institute." She looked at me blankly. "The museum?" I continued.

Diamond White

"Downtown?" She shook her head. "Not even on a school trip?"

"Anyway," she said, "it's cool." She said it in a tone that indicated surprise. I looked down at the white oxford shirt and beige chinos I was wearing. Gap ad with swing dancers. Another era, probably also before she was born. I must have looked like a soccer mom to her.

James limped over from the bookshelf, where he had been perusing my Sue Grafton collection. Maybe trying to learn the alphabet. How long had I left them alone while I was in the kitchen? Well, there really wasn't anything of value to steal. The place was still bare bones. He wore pressed black jeans and a black dress shirt with black buttons. His head was freshly shaved and there were multiple silver studs in both ears, a silver ring through his right eyebrow.

He glanced at the food I had just set on the table, a look of distaste clear on his face.

"I know I'm not your mom," I told him, "but seriously, when did you last eat a vegetable? You look like I could snap you in two."

"I drink Kombucha every day," piped Sherry, who came and plopped herself loosely in one of the mismatched dining chairs.

"And?"

"And so I'm healthy."

"I really don't think that's how it works."

She shrugged, and took a cucumber slice from the tray and popped it in her mouth. James sat heavily next to her, his knee still clearly a source of pain.

"What the hell are we even doing here?" he asked with derision. "Mrs. Right sees us, she'll call the cops."

"You're here because you owe me, and it's time for me to collect."

Diamond White

"We owe you! Look what you did to my knee. I can still barely walk."

"It's a job, and there's money in it."

Sherry leaned forward eagerly. "What do we have to do?"

"How much?" asked James at the same time.

I took a big drink of smoothie, then set my glass on the table, waiting. I looked at Sherry's smoothie, then pointedly at James's. Sherry picked hers up and took a long drink, set it down and wiped her mouth with the back of her hand.

James rolled his eyes. "Jesus H. Christ," he moaned, and took a gulp, his face screwing up at the taste.

"Two thousand dollars each." Both of their eyes widened. "Plus the two thousand in back rent that you owe Mrs. Right."

"What do we have to do?" asked Sherry between bites of salad.

"In cash," demanded James at the same time.

"I'll let you know in a few days' time, when all the details are worked out."

"Are we robbing something?" asked James, his eyes squinting shrewdly. "Your boyfriend said something about diamonds when we was here before."

"No diamonds. No robbery. All you need to do is act tough and pick a fight. Do you think you can do that?"

Sherry snorted, and looked up.

"That," she said, "is James's specialty."

27

I opened my eyes and blinked in the brightness of the spotlight. I squinted, trying to see past it into the surrounding darkness. No good.

I looked down, assessing and testing my restraints. I was tied to a strong wooden dining chair, the kind with arms and a slatted back. My wrists were bound to the arms of the chair with clothesline. I leaned over but couldn't get my teeth anywhere near the knots, because more rope wrapped around my chest and the back of the chair. My feet were likewise bound to the chair legs.

I shook the long black hair out of my eyes and looked to my right. Al Hansen was similarly tied to the exact same style chair, but in addition, he was gagged. He looked sweaty, and was mmphing wildly behind the duct tape plastered across his face.

Next to him, in the exact same predicament, was Jorge Alvarez. The gang's all here.

I looked to my left, and there, tied expertly to a fourth chair, was Jared Dexter. Jared Dexter was having a bad day. No duct tape, but he was trussed like the rest of us. He was also bruised and swollen all over his face. One eye was almost shut, and it looked perhaps like a piece of his ear was missing—the lobe was covered with blood-soaked gauze.

He looked very unhappy.

My attention was diverted by the sound of hard shoes on the concrete floor. A tall man stepped out of the darkness in front of us, stopping about ten feet away. He wore a white lab coat that glared brightly in the spotlight. Black pants and black leather shoes. He had abnormally white-blond hair and gold-rimmed glasses. Disturbingly, he was wearing black latex gloves.

"Miss Wrigley," he addressed me in a low voice. "You're awake."

Diamond White

"What the holy hell is going on!" I shouted. "You can't do this to me!"

"You'll notice you are not gagged, Miss Wrigley."

"I'm a lawyer, I will have you hanged—"

"If you'd like to remain ungagged, I suggest you answer the question I have for you. Your life may well depend on it."

I closed my mouth and glared at him defiantly.

"Excellent. Now, I have only one question, and I want you to answer it, without hesitation, to prove your worth to me."

I tensed against my bonds, but I wasn't going anywhere. The ropes cutting across the top of my chest were tight, as were those on my wrists.

He took a step closer to me, his deep brown eyes staring intently.

"Who supplies the guns for your little start-up business?"

"What are you talking about?" I spat at him. He reached out with a lightning hand and slapped me across the face. I could taste the talc from the latex gloves.

"You are selling guns, lots of guns, in Austin, and Lawndale, other places as well."

I looked at him incredulously.

"Are you nuts? We're buying guns off the street! We aren't selling them to anyone, that's—"

He slapped me again, which I was not enjoying in the least, though I was grateful that the slaps were not as hard as they could have been.

"Silence!" He turned his back on me for a moment, took a few steps to my left. He reached out and pinched Dexter's earlobe between his thumb and forefinger, causing Dexter to howl in pain. The torturer let go, wiped his fingers on his coat, leaving a red smear of blood, and looked at Dexter with a smile.

Diamond White

"Now, who did this to you, Mr. Dexter?"

Jared Dexter looked down and away, not meeting the madman's eyes.

"None of my people, I can tell. My people would never be so messy."

Dexter kept his mouth shut.

"I bet it was somebody who wanted those diamonds..."

Jared Dexter looked up quickly.

"Oh yes," the man continued. "I know all about the diamonds. I know you were supposed to launder them for your Mexican friend. I know he's upset that they have gone missing, I know he is coming here."

"Listen—" began Dexter, but the inquisitor held his finger up to Dexter's lips, causing Dexter to pull his head back in disgust.

"Shhh. I am only interested in you answering the questions I have. And the question I have is: What is the name of your gun supplier in Mexico?"

Dexter didn't answer, so the crazy freak walked back over to me, pointing the gun at my chest.

"Miss Wrigley, do you have an answer?"

At that moment, Al Hansen worked the duct tape away from his mouth enough to speak.

"She doesn't know anything!!" He yelled. "She had nothing to do with it, neither did I!"

"Well, in that case..." He winked at me, then swiveled from me to Al and shot him in the chest.

I screamed, and so did Dexter. Hanson's head slumped forward and blood rand down the front of his shirt in a dark river. Jorge mmphed behind his gag, sweat on his brow.

"Igor!" The man called out over his shoulder, and another man came out of the shadows to stand next to him. He was wearing a black ski mask, black t-shirt and

Diamond White

pants. Black Nikes. "Take Officer Hansen to the waiting room."

Without hesitation, the man in black walked behind Hansen's chair. He tipped it back on two legs, making Hansen's head loll back, and began to drag him backwards into the darkness. Blood trickled from the hole in Hansen's chest, leaving a trail along the cement floor to the place where he disappeared into shadow. The sound of wooden chair legs scraping on concrete continued for another thirty or forty seconds.

I pulled wildly at my bonds, as did the two other remaining captives. Dr. Frankenstein dropped the gun into his lab coat pocket and sauntered back over to me.

"Sure you don't have any information for me?"

He leaned in close, blocking Dexter's view of my face, and gave me another wink.

"You're too pretty to destroy," he said creepily, standing back up to his full height. "I think I'll save you for Igor to play with later." He pulled his left arm back, telegraphing his swing so I saw his open hand coming at my face. At the last minute I pushed hard off the floor with my right foot. This, combined with the force of the slap, tipped the entire chair over to the left, sending me crashing to the floor. I held my neck stiff to make sure my head didn't hit the concrete, then let it slack, pretending I was unconscious.

"Igor!" the man called again.

Igor once again emerged from the shadows. As he approached me, he pulled a switch blade from his back pocket, flicking it open with an ominous "swick." He bent down and cut the ropes binding my chest, wrists, and ankles, causing me to flop out onto the floor. He closed the blade, returned it to his pocket, then picked me up and slung me over his shoulder, the hair of the long black wig hanging down and blocking my face.

Diamond White

We left the circle of light and stepped through a black curtain into a dimly lit hallway, at which point I reached down and grabbed Igor's ass with both hands. He gave a little squeal at the goosing and quickly set me back down on my feet. He took my hand and led me through a door at the end of the hallway, then pulled off his ski mask to reveal the face of Nick Shelby.

"Oh," I said, in faux surprise. "It's you!"

"It's me," he agreed.

"Igor?" I asked. "A little much?"

"Talk to Don, he wrote the script."

"Shhh!" said Al Hansen, who was sitting at a long table watching a monitor. He had taken off his shirt and the squib apparatus underneath, and was wearing a fresh blue button-down Oxford. He reached forward and turned the volume up on the monitor.

"I hope it's clear," Don was saying, "that I am not playing around. You have sixty seconds to tell me what I want to know."

"Wow," I said quietly. "Crazy torturer Don is creepy as hell."

"I know," said Nick, "he's way into it."

"The bleached hair and the voice! He's got a great Christopher Walken vibe going."

On the monitor, Jorge was mmphing and gyrating wildly while Don was giving Dexter the death stare. Finally, he turned and walked over, ripping the duct tape from Jorge's mouth.

"Antonio Negron!" the gang leader blurted. "His name is Antonio Negron."

"Excellent!" exclaimed Don with a big smile. "You get to live!" He turned back to Dexter. "And you do, too, Mr. Dexter, even though you have been incredibly unhelpful."

I could see Dexter's shoulders slump with relief at the news.

155

Diamond White

"Your Mr. Negron has been horning in on my territory," continued Don. "Perhaps he doesn't realize that. Perhaps *you* didn't realize that. I hope you have gotten the message today. I'm sure your associates Miss Wrigley and Officer Hansen got the message.

"I have a message for your boss, and you are going to deliver it. My sources tell me that he is coming here soon, because his diamonds are missing, and it has led him to wonder if he has misplaced his trust in you."

"But it wasn't my fault—"

"I know it wasn't," said Don, pulling a small felt pouch from his lab coat pocket. "I know because I have the diamonds right here."

Dexter's eyes widened in disbelief.

"You are dealing with a power greater than you can possibly comprehend," said Don smoothly, laying it on thick. "You are going to convince Mr. Negron to meet with me, at a time and place of my choosing."

"I don't—"

"If the meeting goes well, I will return Mr. Negron's diamonds, and we will perhaps do business together."

He turned on his heel and walked over to Jorge. He returned the diamonds to his pocket, withdrawing a cell phone and, from the other pocket, the gun. He laid the gun in Jorge's lap.

"Here, hold this for me a moment, would you?" He took the phone and put it in the breast pocket of Jorge's white t-shirt. Jorge looked at the gun, tantalizingly close in his lap, but out of reach of his bound hands. He opened his mouth to speak, but Don just shook his head.

"Shush, little gangster. I don't know how big or small your role in this whole thing is, but selling guns to rival gangs means you have no soul. Therefore, I have a special job for you. Ready?"

Jorge nodded his head.

Diamond White

"From now until I meet with Mr. Negron, you are Mr. Dexter's shadow. If he does anything you think I wouldn't like, you call me."

"Now wait just a minute!" Dexter objected.

Don picked up the gun and pointed it straight at Jared Dexter's face.

"Or, my friend, you can just shoot him instead. *Comprendes*?" He lowered the gun and dropped it back into Jorge's lap.

"*Si*," said Jorge in a defeated voice.

Don turned on his heel, walking toward the waiting ring of darkness.

"Goodbye gentleman," he called over his shoulder. "You will hear from me soon."

On his way out of the room he flicked a switch on the wall, and the spotlight went out, a glowing red afterimage dancing in the vision of the two men left alone, bound, in the darkness.

28

"He didn't even call the police!" I said indignantly to Ruby, as we kayaked around the lake. Ruby wasn't big on exercise, but she couldn't think of a good excuse when I introduced kayaking. Her bad leg was no hindrance to an afternoon of paddling.

The sky was bright blue, and there was a light, cool breeze blowing across the surface of the lake. All along the banks, oak and maple trees were ablaze with the yellow and orange of autumn. We had been at it since lunch, and had barely seen another person on the water.

"Sure, it was too late for Hansen, but I was supposedly still alive. In fact, Don pretty much said he was going to haul me off for torture and rape, and the guy doesn't even call the police."

"It's this Negron," said Ruby, frowning as she paddled. Over the course of the last two hours, she had lost all her awkwardness in the kayak, and was now proceeding like a pro. I had to work to keep up. Ruby never did anything by half. "If all your enemies are so afraid of him, are you sure meeting with him is a good plan? I know you're in pretty good hands with Elgort, but still..."

"You're not wrong, Ruby. Dexter has barely shown his face in the two days since we released him. According to Earl, the mayor still hasn't been able to find him, which means Dexter is lying really low. We've only heard from Jorge once so far, and that was just a quick text to say all was well."

Ruby chuckled. "I bet he didn't like being called 'little gangster.'"

"Not at all, but he stuck to the script."

"I find it odd," Ruby mused, laying the paddle across the kayak and coasting as we made our way back up the canal to the cabin. "You're a good woman, who's become a criminal. And you're surrounded by bad people, who are trying to become better. It's an odd match-up."

"Not Earl," I countered. "Or Park. She's like me. A former rule follower."

"Speaking of the devil," said Ruby.

I looked up. We were only about fifty yards from the dock, now, and standing on it, waving cheerfully to us, was Ellery Park. I looked at her and my heart lurched.

"Ruby," I said, "we've got to get her out of here and into law school somewhere. Somewhere far away. Promise me?"

"Pinkie swear," she said, holding her right pinkie out toward my left hand, which, of course, had no pinkie.

"Nice."

"That joke, it never gets old," said Ruby, cracking herself up.

My left hand still had a middle finger, though, which I put to good use.

"So then I go all the way up to the twenty-fifth floor," Park was telling us over coffee on the front porch, as we watched the sun go down, "and Miss Archer herself comes out and invites me to her office. She is amazing! Like, you can feel the power just coming off her in waves. And great clothes. She just exudes strength. And her office!" Park gestured horizontally with her arm. "Windows, all the way across!"

"El—"

"Yup, of course. Sorry." She took a big drink, draining the last of her coffee, which I was beginning to think was a bad idea if she was going to be this hyper. "She's pretty sure, based on what we got out of Dexter's phone while he was unconscious, that she's isolated Negron's phone. And, if she's right, then Negron landed at O'Hare this morning."

Diamond White

"That's great! Then we're on. I'll let Don know, and he can set up the meeting." Park beamed. "But," I added, "you didn't have to drive all the way up here to tell me that."

"No, but I brought all the stuff Marty made for you. Or his people made for you. It's in my car. I thought you might want to practice with it before the big showdown."

"Thanks, but El, seriously, what the hell happened in Florida?" Her black eye had turned a repulsive yellowish green.

"A hurricane happened!" grimaced Park, looking as surly as I'd ever seen her. "You sent me into a hurricane! And then it just got worse!"

Oops. Guess I should have looked at the weather more closely.

"So, you didn't bring me any Butterbeer, then?"

"No," she responded through tight lips, "I did not."

"When did you see Martin?" asked Ruby, changing the subject.

Park blushed. Oh crap. Law school. Hawaii maybe. We had to save this girl from getting too enmeshed in this life of crime we had built.

"I just stopped in to say hi, after I left the Farnham Building. He said he was terribly busy, so I offered to bring you the stuff."

"Relax," I told her. "Ruby's just messing with you."

El looked hesitantly at Ruby. "It's me you have to worry about," I added. She swiveled back to me quickly.

"Are, are you and Marty? I mean—I didn't mean to, not with..." I let her sputter to a stop.

"Of course I'm not," I said, laughing. She and Ruby both started to frown. "Not that he isn't a great guy, and handsome, but we're just friends. He's ten years younger than me, after all."

Park's little jaw dropped. "You're thirty-four?"

161

Diamond White

Now it was my turn to frown. "I can't tell if you're impressed or horrified."

"I thought you were twenty-five, twenty-eight at the most. You look incredible."

Now I blushed.

"Aw shucks, El. You just earned yourself a dinner invitation."

"Which," said Ruby, levering herself up out of her chair and collecting the coffee cups, "I will go make."

"Do you need help with the cooking?" asked Park.

"Not for about forty years now," said Ruby without looking back, "since I first got married."

Park and I looked at each other in shock.

"Ruby," I started to ask, but she had timed her exit line perfectly, and the door had already shut behind her.

A story for another time, it seemed.

29

El and I stood with Marty in the Art Institute of Chicago,
looking at the Chagall Window. It was 3 a.m. With the
lobby lights off, but the backing lights on, the stained
glass was more beautiful than ever. My mother would
have bemoaned the fact that natural light no longer
shone through the panes, but she would have loved the
vibrancy that the restoration had brought to them.

"Ahem," coughed Marty, quietly, and I snapped out of
my trance.

"Right! We've got to get out of here, I know. I just
can't come to the Institute without visiting these
windows."

"Even at night," added Park.

"When not a creature is stirring," I said.

"And the guards are asleep," Marty chimed in.

"And the cameras are off," I concluded.

We turned and headed back the way we had come.

"Is it safe to open the doors?" Park asked.

"Yes," Marty answered, "everything's down, but we
don't want to go out the front, obviously."

"Back the way we came in?" I suggested.

"Yes, that'll work," Marty agreed.

"This is so strange," said Park as our footsteps echoed.
"Like we're the only ones left alive on the planet."

"*Night of the Comet,*" said Marty.

"Holy crap, Martin. Do you not watch any movie made
after 1990?"

"I do, but I am a student of the eighties. It will be our
most studied decade, from a cultural standpoint, mark my
words."

Park looked back and forth between us, then smiled.

"What?" we both said to her at the same time.

"Riley's right, you two are like siblings."

"Great," I moaned.

Diamond White

Marty beamed. "Can I call you Sis? Big Sis?"

"Only if you want to die..."

An hour earlier, we launched this operation in preparation for our meeting with Negron. We had decided the Institute was the perfect place: Negron would have no upper hand, but would also assume that we didn't have the upper hand either. We were counting on it.

First, I freeclimbed the back side of the Museum while Park kept a lookout, and Marty looked for the security WiFi. While building the new wing, they had replaced the miles and miles of coaxial cable for the security cameras with digital cameras wirelessly connected to a network. A lot easier to maintain, but a lot more vulnerable as well.

The climbing wasn't as hard as I thought it would be; there was a secluded area in the corner, away from the new Modern Wing, and good handholds all the way up. I was wearing beige tights and a turtleneck, with a matching ski mask, to blend with the color of the stone wall. I couldn't find a beige fannypack, so we spray painted one. It was already flaking off, but it didn't have to last long.

Marty had given Park all the gizmos I asked for, but at the last minute he decided he wanted to come along. I couldn't tell if he was being protective of El, or if he was just tired of being cooped up in his office. What's the point of making cool stuff if you don't get to try it out yourself?

I scuttled across the roof, then climbed quietly down into McKinlock Court. This was the most dangerous part, when I was most visible, but I made it without incident. I lay on my back, flat on the ground; pressed hard up against the interior wall, I was nearly invisible.

Diamond White

I surveilled the courtyard carefully, looking for guards and security cameras. None of the first, plenty of the second.

I waited. My iPhone was taped to the small of my back. It was agreed that Marty would send me vibrating texts to alert me when it was time to move to the next part of the plan. As I lay there, I pictured Marty on the outside of the wall, typing furiously on his keyboard, and it brought me back to the day I lost my fingers. Aldo Frances had locked a bomb around my wrist, and Marty had worked frantically to try to diffuse it, putting his life in terrible danger the entire time.

The phone buzzed once against my back. The cameras were off. I rolled onto my stomach and crawled along the wall to the corner. I was about to make a move toward the closest door when I spotted the first guard, only a few yards away!

He was sitting at one of the outdoor café tables, smoking a cigarette, earbuds trailing from his ears into his shirt pocket. He was heavy set, Middle Eastern-looking, and clearly bored. Was he listening to music? The news? Language lessons?

He was so motionless I might have thought he was dead if the end of his cigarette didn't pulse orange each time he took a drag. The umbrella for the table had completely hidden him when I looked down from the roof. I had gotten lucky.

Now it was time to test one of the first gizmos, and I eased it out of my pack. I had asked Marty to make a knock-out spray. How hard could that be, right? You see them in spy movies all the time. Turns out those movies may not be totally accurate. Like knocking people out with a karate chop or a truncheon. Generally, people don't just drop to the ground unconscious. They scream, and yell, and bleed, and roll around on the ground. I

Diamond White

wanted the knock-out spray to work like in the movies, but it turns out that wasn't quite as simple as it looked either.

Instead of something like a can of mace, I had a little gas mask attached to a round rubber bladder like you would have on a kid's bike horn. Marty said a spray wouldn't be concentrated enough. Trouble was, you had to hold the mask over the target's mouth and nose for about ten seconds. Then, they'd be out for an hour or more. Ten seconds, that wasn't going to be easy.

Sneaking up behind guard number one, however, was a snap. Whatever he was listening to, he had it turned up loud. I moved slowly until I was right behind him, and waited for the instant he pulled the cigarette from his mouth to tap the ash. I clamped the mask over his face, squeezing the bulb and pulling backward at the same time until his chair overturned and his head almost cracked on the pavers. I went down on my knees, pushing them into his chest with all my weight, trapping his face and the mask between my shins and thighs. I caught one hand by the wrist as he raised it to try and ward me off. His other hand groped for his belt— no gun, but he had a walkie-talkie. I leaned forward and grabbed it from its holder before he could find it.

I was at about five Mississippi, and he was flopping like a beached whale, but with his legs up in the air and my weight on his torso, he couldn't get any leverage.

At seven Mississippi he started to fade and by ten, just like Marty promised, he was out. I rolled him under the table, stood up, and righted the chair. I took the used plunger bulb off the mask, and swapped it for a fresh one from my pack. I also retrieved my lock pick set and headed quickly for the door.

A few moments later I was opening the service entrance to the museum's café; Marty and El slipped in

Diamond White

quietly. Marty opened his shoulder bag and handed me eight small disks made of pink plastic. They looked exactly like air fresheners. I held one up to my nose; they even smelled like air fresheners. They were actually remote WiFi disruptors, and would allow Marty to turn the cameras on and off without having to hack into the system again. I slipped them into my pack, then held out my hand to El, motioning for her to give me the large backpack she was carrying. She slid it off her shoulders and handed it to me.

"Okay," I whispered. "Meet at the Chagall window in thirty minutes. And stick together." I needed to make sure Park would keep Marty safe. I wanted to take him with me, but I was heading into the more dangerous area of the museum.

My first stop was the Impressionists. Always one of Mom's favorites. If I had a dollar for every time I stood in front of that Caillebotte, well, I'd have a lot of dollars. I crossed the lower level without incident, placing one of the disks on the underside of the staircase before heading up.

Cautiously, I made my way to the front of the building. From beside the grand staircase I could see into the lobby, where the guard at the front desk seemed to be slumped over. I was bewildered. Marty and El couldn't possibly have gotten here before me. I watched carefully as his chest rose and fell, his hands joined on his considerable gut. My God, he was asleep. Well, that saves me some of the knock-out gas. I placed the disruptor in an inconspicuous spot and headed upstairs to the second floor, moving slowly and peering over the top of the staircase.

This is where my luck would end. Strolling through the Impressionists, heading my way, was a very tall young man. No headphones, wide awake; he actually seemed to

Diamond White

be looking at the art! Probably a graduate student at the Institute who took this job as a way to earn money and get some studying in.

I kept my head down until he stopped to look at "Sunday in the Park," his back to me as he examined the painting close up. I slid the pack off my back and set it on the steps. From the fanny pack I got out the knockout gas, but I couldn't figure out how I was going to get the mask on his face—the guy was about fourteen inches taller than me. Fortunately, he also looked like he weighed about 160 pounds. He was thinner than most of my excuses.

I reached into the small front pocket of the backpack and found a penny. Watching the back of his head, I waited until he was looking to the right of the frame, then pitched the penny as hard as I could through the entryway on his left, into the room with the Van Gogh in it.

Ping!

That snapped him out of his studies. He put his hand on his radio, reflexively, but did not take it out of its holster. He must have decided to check it out on his own first, and headed into the other room.

I scrambled up the last few stairs, moving silently across the floor in my flexible rock-climbing shoes, turning and sitting on my heels with my back to the wall, just under the painting the guard had been staring at only moments ago. I stilled my breath, then looked down to check that the gas mask was still attached to the squeeze bulb and ready to go. I heard his hard shoes on the floor as he returned. Still no call to anyone else.

I glanced up toward the corner of the ceiling, where a camera stared back blankly. The fact that no alarm had sounded yet was confirmation that Marty's gizmos were effective. That would cause its own problem, though, and

168

soon. I figured the guards in the control room would spend about ten minutes, tops, banging the sides of the monitors and checking all the connections before they called someone in tech services for help. Well before then, according to the plan, Marty and El would have located the control room and run sleeping gas in under the door jamb. I was going to assume that their part of the plan was going just fine, unless I heard otherwise, likely in the form of police sirens.

The footsteps drew closer as Tall and Skinny made his way back toward my position. I straightened my back against the wall, still in a crouch. I shifted all my weight onto my left foot, and leaned so far to the left that I put my left palm down on the floor for extra leverage.

And three, two, one...

He stepped into the room, first his left foot and then his right. While his right foot was still in the air, I lashed out sideways and hard with my right foot, stomping sideways into and through his left foot. His foot shot out from under him, and he went down hard on his left side. I reached out and caught his head before it hit the marble floor, my left hand cradled underneath and my right hand clamping the mask over his nose and mouth. As I had done with bachelor number one downstairs, I turned my body and sat down heavily on his chest, trapping his arms between my knees.

His howl of pain was mostly muffled by the mask, and now he grunted mightily as he tried to buck me off in a panic. The poor guy was terrified, with no idea what was happening to him. Plus, I'd probably broken his left ankle. "Sorry buddy," I thought with one part of my brain while the other part counted seven, eight, nine... and his eyes glazed over.

I jumped up, grabbing the mask from his face and hurrying back to the staircase for the backpack. Carefully,

Diamond White

I took the Degas sculpture, the one from Dexter's office, out of the bag and hurried into the next room.

A huge painting of a man and a woman, walking down a rainy Parisian street, hung on the wall. There's the Caillebotte, Mom, I thought to myself. Can't stay and stare at it right now. The full-size Degas sculpture stood in the middle of the floor. It was heartbreakingly beautiful: a young dancer posed to begin, her body made of bronze, but her clothes real clothes of cotton, slightly shabby all these decades later.

As part of a special exhibit, seven low pedestals had been set around the room, each bearing one of Degas' foot-tall studies. I moved quickly to the one that most resembled the one in my hands, then stopped short. I looked at the Caillebotte on the wall. Surely it had some sort of trigger alarm that would go off if anyone tried to remove the painting. Definitely. It was the number one reason I wasn't considering taking it home with me. Would the little sculptures be alarmed as well? Only one way to find out.

I stood in front of the pedestal, holding Dexter's statue heavily in one hand, weighing it against the statue in front of me. I took a few deep breaths to psyche myself up and then, before I could think better of it, I switched them in one quick movement.

I waited, the statue heavy in my hand, but no alarms went off.

Quickly, I made my way back to the stairs and grabbed the backpack, carefully putting the genuine statue in and throwing it over my shoulder as I made my way back through Impressionism, past the sleeping guard, and down to the end of the hall to the women's room. Looking into the Modern Wing, I could see another security guard strolling the floor, but he was heading away from me into the galleries. No point picking a fight.

Diamond White

I pushed into the women's room and entered the first stall. I peeled down the athletic tights I was wearing, and sat down and peed. I really should have gone beforehand.

I reached back and carefully unstuck the iPhone from my back, texting Marty: all clear. He sent back a smiley face emoji, one eye winking open and closed. I assumed that meant good news.

I wiped myself and worked the stretchy pants back up over my hips, thought better of flushing. At the sink, I took a moment to look at myself in the mirror, and then broke out laughing. It was 3 a.m. in Chicago, and I was prowling around the Art Institute.

My life had never been so strange, or so exciting.

I ran off to meet up with Ellery and Marty, who were probably making out in front of the Chagall window.

30

"I am never getting on that thing with you again," moaned Nick, standing hunched over with his hands on his knees.

"Breathe deep, my friend. You'll be just fine." I patted him on the back. "I'll go in and get our food, you just take it easy."

When I said the word "food," I think he started to heave, but then held it down. By the time I came out of the Lucky Platter with the bag of takeout, he was standing up straight and looking much less green.

"Let's leave Gromet here and walk to the lake," I said, patting the motorcycle on the gas tank as I passed by it.

"Yes, let's," Nick agreed.

We had cruised over to Evanston to have a nice little pre-evil-mastermind-showdown dinner without the likelihood of being recognized. I had insisted on taking the motorcycle, even though Nick hadn't been very enthusiastic about it. The weather was absolutely beautiful. Nick took the rolled-up blanket off the back of the seat and gamely followed me down the sidewalk, stopping to look in the window of a used book shop.

In a few minutes, we came to a good-sized park on the lake, the cool wind whipping through our short hair— mine was only slightly longer than his—as we strode across the grass to a spot by the water.

"Here?" he asked, indicating the grassy ground.

"Sure."

With a shrug of his long arms he unfurled the dark green blanket, straightening the edges once it was stretched on the ground. I put down the bag and drew out the tandoori chicken salad and the crab cakes.

"So," said Nick after we were settled and digging into the food, "not to talk shop, but are you ready for tomorrow?"

173

Diamond White

"I think so," I said, and I actually meant it.

"Well you made the morning news, that's for sure."

"Yes, and without my underwear showing for a change," I said, referring to an embarrassing incident from last spring.

He laughed. "That's right. I almost forgot."

The break-in at the Art Institute the night before had caused quite a stir, especially with the scheduled visit tomorrow of the Vice President of Zambia, who would be visiting the African Art gallery and then discussing a trade deal with Senator Durbin over lunch in McKinlock Court. Six guards had been incapacitated by what were assumed to be multiple assailants, and even more troubling was the fact that the surveillance cameras had been deactivated by a very clever hacker. Strangest of all was the fact that nothing had been taken. Nothing at all.

The news anchor was unaware, and well he should be, that on the other end of the museum, in the auditorium on the second floor of the Modern Wing, another meeting was planned for noon tomorrow as well. This one would be between Antonio Negron and Alden Earl, the subject of which would be the future sales and distribution of weapons throughout parts of Chicago. Earl, with the help of Uncle Elgort and family, would attempt to dissuade Negron from doing any further business in the city. As I mentioned before, the Art Institute presented itself as a level playing field, a place in which Negron would not feel threatened. Right up to the point when we began threatening him.

It had been my job to unlevel the playing field, if there is such a phrase.

"I'm happy to report," I said, smiling mischievously at my dinner companion, "that the Chicago Police, in conjunction with the museum security staff, will be taking the unprecedented step of searching all bags of visitors when they enter tomorrow, and each visitor will also be subjected to a metal detection wand to ensure that no weapons of any kind are brought into the museum."

Nicky gave me an impressed whistle. I bowed my head.

"Thank you, thank you! Also, computer experts are working around the clock to improve the computer firewalls so as to protect the security cameras from any further outside hacking."

"Outside hacking?"

"Right."

"So that's a little bit of closing the barn door, isn't it?"

"The what?"

"The barn door," he said, wiping his mouth with a napkin.

"What the hell are you talking about?"

"It's a saying. Closing the barn door after the horse is already out."

"I've never heard that, sorry."

He waved it away.

"My fault. You spend too much time with Uncle Elgort and you start to feel like you live in a different century. I swear Don thinks it's 1962."

I laughed. "Does he ever do anything for fun?"

"He plays fantasy baseball."

I frowned, picturing Don in wool trousers and holding a fat mitt. "Like reenactments?"

"No," Nick laughed again. He should laugh more. "It's a game where you have a team made up of real players, and you get points for their stats. You pick the best players, you win a lot of money."

"That's basically the stock market," I mused.

"Yes, I'm afraid so. His fun is pretty much the same as his work."

"We've got to get him a girlfriend," I suggested.

Diamond White

"I don't think so."

"Or boyfriend," I added hastily. "Whatever is cool."

"No, it's not that, it's just that he sees a lot of women, but never seems interested in taking it further. I'm pretty sure my brother intends to stay a bachelor."

"What he should really do," I said, wiping ketchup off my fingers, "is join an acting troupe. He Christopher Walkened the living daylights out of me in that warehouse. I bet Dexter crapped his pants." I gathered up all the trash and consolidated it into one bag.

"Don is good at everything he puts his hand to, always has been. He just seems to like numbers the best."

"Well," I said, snuggling up to him, "you seem pretty good at everything, too." The sun had dropped behind the buildings and it was getting chilly. Nick put his arm around me and squeezed me tightly.

"Thanks," he said, resting his chin on the top of my head. "I know a few tricks."

"I'll vouch for that," I said, digging my fingers into his ribs and instigating a tickle fight.

Moments later we were on our backs, side by side, breathless from laughing.

"I'm going to lose my dinner," said Nick gasping.

"You haven't even gotten on the bike yet," I teased.

"Oh God," he groaned, and I started to tickle him again.

"What do you mean we aren't going to be there!" roared Ruby, slamming a pot down on the kitchen counter of my apartment.

"That's ridiculous," chimed in Park. "It's not fair, it's—"

"Bullshit!" yelled Ruby. "It is bullshit, and you know it."

"Keep your voice down, please. Mrs. Right will hear you."

Diamond White

She stomped over to the sofa and sat down hard. Park moved over to the side table to examine the small Degas dancer.

"Oof. This couch, it has no cushion!"

"It's Modernist," I answered.

"The people who lived here before," Ruby complained, looking around, "they had no taste. Nothing matches."

Standing in the middle of the room, I put my hands on my hips and looked around.

"I bought all this furniture, Ruby. I picked it out. It's mine."

She pursed her lips, looking around. "*Prominte*. I didn't realize." Her voice was now at a normal volume. "But it's all a hodgepodge! Your other apartment, everything matched. Why this?"

"I don't know Ruby. I wanted everything to be different. I wanted to see something I liked and grab for it, instead of following all the regulations. I don't want to look at any part of my life anymore and think it's a lie."

"Except your secret identity," put in Park, sitting down next to Ruby.

"What?"

"You want to live an authentic life, but you're dead and have two aliases, that I know of."

"What's your point?"

"I...I don't know," admitted Park, "except that you should stop telling us what to do. You're making crazy decisions for yourself every day, then don't want us to make crazy decisions on our own."

"Yes!" crowed Ruby. "Yes, you do as you do and not as you say. I mean—"

"I get it," I sighed. I was feeling ganged up on, and started pacing the floor. "It's really Uncle Elgort's plan, I'm just one little part of it."

Ruby rose to her feet, Park following.

"Fine. We will go and talk to Mr. Elgort Shelby about getting on his payroll."

"No, really. My part's pretty much done, now. *Nick* isn't even going to be there tomorrow."

"I will talk to him anyway," Ruby persisted, heading for the door.

"No, I prom—"

She stopped with her hand on the door, Park nearly running into the back of her.

"You what?"

"Nothing!"

"You promised what?"

"Nothing, no—"

"Who!"

I stood there, not saying anything, chewing my lip and fidgeting from foot to foot.

"Kay Colleen Riley," Ruby spoke through gritted teeth.

My shoulders collapsed.

"Marty. I promised Marty I'd keep you out of things."

Instinctively I held my hands up to ward off an attack, but it didn't come.

"Me too?" Park demanded, but she could see the answer in my face.

When I raised my head and lowered my hands, Ruby was just standing there looking at me. Finally, she spoke.

"You're my best friend, Kay, but you don't get to tell me what to do, and neither does Martin."

"I'm sorry."

She opened the door and pushed Park through it, then stepped through after her. "Come up to the lake when it's all over," she said, and closed the door.

Crap.

31

The next morning, I did an hour of stretches, followed by a five-mile run. I freaking hate jogging. I cooled off by performing a few taekwondo poomses, followed by some more stretching, then a long, hot shower. When the doorbell rang at 10:45 I was struggling to get my new motorcycle leathers on over my clothes; I usually just wore underwear underneath. I looked down at my feet: I was wearing a pair of nondescript black Merrill shoes that I hoped could function as both business casual and biker chic. I looked in the mirror at my hair, which last night I had dyed bright blond. I shrugged. This was going to be quite a day.

I trotted down the stairs and opened the door for James and Sherry, who were also dressed in motorcycle leathers.

"C'mon in," I said. And then, "You're going to have to remove those chains," pointing at the numerous chains on James's belt and boots. He frowned. "You'll set off the detectors," I explained. "Have you had breakfast?"

They both just rolled their eyes.

Ninety minutes later, we were on the second floor of the Modern Wing at the Institute. James looked uncomfortable, but couldn't stop looking up at the amazing architecture. He seemed to not even register the art. As we rounded the corner, Sherry stopped short and caught her breath, staring at the Jackson Pollock.

"Shit," she said, then clamped her hand over her mouth, looking around furtively. Not like everyone wasn't looking at us anyway. We were the only ones in the gallery, and likely the museum, dressed head to toe in black leather.

"I thought you'd want to see it in real life," I said, feeling like a proud teacher.

Diamond White

"It's pretty awesome," she admitted, then stepped closer. "Hey, look," she said, turning her head to look at the canvas from an angle. "It's all three-dimensional, you can see the drips."

I smiled again. If we all died in the next hour, at least I would have introduced a young person to Modern Art. Mom would be proud.

Out of the corner of my eye I saw Uncle Elgort moving slowly along the outer hallway, pausing now and then to lean on his cane and look up at the glass ceiling. Security had closed all entrances except for the main front doors, even for staff, so Elgort had to pass through the metal detector and then make his slow way to the far end of the building.

"C'mon," I motioned to my two henchmen, "we've got to get into position."

We walked briskly back through the building until we reached the Impressionist corridor once again. I counted three guards just in these few rooms: two security personnel, and a regular Chicago cop, called in to ensure the safety of the Senator and the Deputy Emir.

The cop gave us a dirty look, and I instinctually slid my damaged hand into my pocket. Likely he just hated bikers, but I didn't want to leave too good of a description behind, even with the blond hair. We wandered around looking at the paintings.

We didn't have to wait long. Five minutes later Jared Dexter and Jorge Alvarez came up the stairs. Alvarez was wearing chinos and a blue oxford shirt that didn't quite cover the tattoos crawling up his neck and down his forearms. Dexter was wearing a grey suit and dark glasses. I'm guessing he still had the remains of the shiner Selena gave him. They were followed conspicuously by six large men in black suits. The men looked strong, and they looked unhappy.

Diamond White

Crap. Six. I was hoping for three or four, max. Whelp! Here we go...

I nodded toward James and Sherry, motioned toward the men with my eyes, though they must have figured out on their own that this was our target. I moved over near the staircase, and pressed my finger three times to the small pink disruptor that was hidden there, perfectly disguised as an air freshener. That would activate all the disruptors in the museum, shutting down the cameras for at least three minutes.

Sherry took a step away from James, who yelled "Hey!" and grabbed her by the arm. She yanked her arm away, causing it to flail backwards, resulting in the back of her hand slapping across the face of the nearest man in black, raking her sharp ring across his cheek and drawing blood.

"Christ!" the man bellowed, and they all turned to look at him as James launched himself, leaping onto the man and grabbing and pulling both the man's ears. They went down in a heap, James yelling all the time.

"That's my girlfriend, you prick!"

At that moment, Jorge made a quick move with his left hand, so fast I didn't see what he did. I know he didn't have any metal weapons, but whatever his tactic was, it was ruthlessly effective. One of the men screamed in pain, grabbing his stomach, and went down on the floor. The remaining henchmen looked rapidly between James and Jorge, wondering who to attack first.

Without missing a beat, Jorge grabbed Dexter—who was looking panicky and lost—by the upper arm and hauled him out of the room and down the hall toward European Art.

"Stop!" yelled a voice and the cop burst into the room, the two security guards also converging on the space.

Diamond White

I took off from my spot on the other side of the hall, launching a flying sidekick at the back of one of the six big men. My soft shoes gave him no warning, and he went down like a ton of bricks. I kept my forward momentum and landed on my feet, running past the smaller security guard, skipping to the side to avoid his grasp. He turned to follow me, but the shouts from behind made him turn back. The cop had already drawn his gun, and was shouting at everyone to stop moving.

I smiled as I sprinted down the hall. I bet those suits weren't used to leaving their guns in the car! I felt a little bad for James and Sherry, who would likely be arrested, but hey, they owed me. Maybe Alden Earl could pull some strings and get them out of trouble.

I hit the women's room at full speed, kicking off my Merrill's as I entered a stall, tripping and nearly bashing my head on the back of the toilet. It was torturous to wriggle out of the leather jacket and pants, especially with the clothes I had on underneath. Finally, the clock ticking louder in my head, I stepped out of the stall, grabbing my shoes and slipping them on my feet. I shoved my leathers into the trash under the sink. I wondered briefly how often they emptied the trash, and if I would have a chance to retrieve them. My grey pantsuit, which I had been wearing, uncomfortably, underneath the leathers, was horribly wrinkled, but I doubt the men would even notice. The wig, which had been pressed against my stomach, was also somewhat the worse for wear, but I arranged it the best I could, gave Georgette Wrigley the once over in the mirror, and headed back out into the museum.

I walked as briskly as possible back to gallery 201, which was for the moment deserted. Apparently, the thugs had decided to go quietly, rather than cause an international incident, and they, the cop, the security

Diamond White

guard, and James and Sherry had all gone off toward administration.

I glanced in all directions to make sure I was alone, then I ran to the little Degas dancer and turned it on its side, yanking on the bottom. Nothing happened.

Crap! I spun around, looking at the other small figures. Had I gotten myself turned around? Crap, oh crap. Choose wisely, I told myself as I rushed to the next one, painfully aware of the ticking clock. The cameras would come back on line any second.

The next one was definitely the right one. I turned it on its side and grasped the base, which came off easily in my hand. I tilted the statue upright, and the gun I had hidden there two nights ago slid out onto the pedestal.

I hate guns. I know, I'm a former cop. I'm an outlaw. But, I just hate them. No time for that, though. I scooped it up and put it in the waistband of my suit pants, covering it with my suit coat. I slapped the bottom back on the statue and set it back upright on the pedestal.

Three seconds later I was striding calmly out of the gallery as an older couple strolled in. Sweat was rolling down my back, but I was keeping a cool expression and my pace was purposeful but measured. I was concentrating so hard that I almost walked straight into a man who was seated on a bench, sketching a Cézanne.

"Hey, Georgette," he said, "have a seat."

I looked down with surprise, straight into the handsome face of Nicholas Shelby. "I... what..."

He took my hand and pulled me down onto the bench. "Shhh," he said softly, all the while his other hand kept sketching the basket of apples.

"What are you doing here!" I said through clenched teeth.

"I thought more about what you said about a level playing field."

Diamond White

"I'm not going to be able to focus if you get caught in the middle of a fight."

"Not me," he said gently. "I'm out of here as soon as Negron goes by. Here." He handed me two of his colored pencils.

"Really?" I glanced sideways at him.

"Screw off the erasers. The red one is a blow gun. The green one is full of needles."

"You are shitting me," I said, accidently raising my voice.

"They aren't poison or anything, but they are six inches long and razor sharp; they'll make a person stop and think when they get hit by one."

I carefully unscrewed the eraser off the green one and peered inside, I could just see the tips of half a dozen needles.

"How'd you get these past the metal detectors?" I whispered.

"They're carbon fiber," he answered, with a very self-satisfied grin on his face. I reached up to touch it, but he grabbed my hand away.

"Head down," he hissed.

I did as he said, concentrating on the sketch in his lap as I counted the legs, all in black dress pants, walking past toward the Modern Wing. Ten sets. Oh man. I had taken six out of the picture, but there were still nine left, plus Negron himself, of course.

"I gotta go," I said, squeezing Nick's hand.

"Be careful," he told me.

Really, you think?

32

I strode behind Negron and his entourage as they made their way down the second-floor balcony to the entrance of the auditorium. I had the two pencils in the breast pocket of my suit coat, and the revolver still tucked into my waist band. There were ten of them. I assumed they were unarmed, but how could I be sure?I hoped things wouldn't get out of hand. Outside the room they stopped, grouping together and conversing in Spanish, which I'm ashamed to admit I speak very little of.

One of them caught my eye as I passed them, lifting his eyebrow in surprise as I opened the door and entered the auditorium. Too bad. Guess they expected boys only. The seats were empty, but up front a long table had been set up with eight chairs arranged around it. In the center of the table was a pitcher of water and a circle of glasses. At one end of the table sat Uncle Elgort, with Don on his right, and Jared Dexter, looking decidedly pale, to the right of Don.

Just as I made it to Uncle Elgort's side, the door opened behind me and the men entered. I made a scene of hugging Elgort hello, placing the revolver in his lap as I did. He moved it swiftly into the pocket of the tweed blazer he was wearing. Then we all stood as the newcomers approached.

A tall man with close-cropped brown hair stepped forward. He had a salt and pepper mustache and was a bit thinner than the others, also a bit better dressed. My eye was drawn to the sparkling rings on his fingers, and what looked like a very stylish watch on his wrist.

"*Hola*," he addressed himself to Uncle Elgort. "I am Antonio Negron. You are Mr. Earl?"

"No," said Elgort, taking his hand in a fragile shake. He suddenly looked about ninety-five years old, standing next to this vibrant opponent. "As Mr. Earl is our

185

Diamond White

respectable public face, we thought it best to keep a, what do they call it, a firewall, between him and any associates that may cause scrutiny." Negron straightened and frowned at this. "My name," Elgort continued, "is Ethan Allen."

I smirked, then caught Don's glare across the table. Also glaring at me was Jared Dexter, apparently realizing that I hadn't suffered any permanent damage from my interrogation at the hands of Crazy Don. Once he put that together, he swiveled to look more closely at Don, glancing up at his dark hair, putting two and two together.

"I assure you, Mr. Allen, that Mr. Earl has nothing to worry about in meeting with me. My credentials are impeccable, my name signifies trustworthiness and honesty throughout all my dealings in the United States and in my home country."

"And yet you manage to provide so many illegal firearms to our citizenry." Again, Negron's face clouded. "I am most interested to learn more about your operation during your brief stay here," Elgort said.

"Brief?" asked Negron.

"Sir..." interjected Dexter.

"Quiet," said Don and Negron at the same time, Don getting to his feet. "I'm sorry, sir, my name is Francis Eldon, I am Mr. Allen and Mr. Earl's executive assistant, and as such I will be running this meeting. Please, have a seat," he indicated the chair at the other end of the table from Elgort, who sat slowly back down in his own chair, leaning his cane up against the edge of the table.

"But sir..." said Dexter, trying again to interject.

"Later," Negron said dismissively.

"I'm sorry," Don said, looking around. "Shall I call for more chairs? We didn't realize you would bring such a large retinue," he added, looking around at the big men.

Diamond White

"Actually," replied Negron in an even voice, "I seem to have misplaced some of my associates. You wouldn't know anything about that, would you?"

"No, I'm afraid not. It's a very strange day. We chose this location thinking it would be unthreatening to you and safe to us, and instead we find the place full of politicians and police."

"I hear also there was a robbery," said a man next to Negron, the first of his henchman to speak. On closer scrutiny, he was a few inches shorter than the others, and a few decades older. Both he and Negron seemed to be about fifty years old. His accent was heavier than his boss's, and his eyes darted quickly around the table, assessing risk.

"Yes, unprecedented. Hopefully nothing too important missing. Chairs?" Don offered again, trying to move things along.

"No thank you, Mr. Allen, we will be fine."

"Eldon."

"Pardon?"

"It's Francis Eldon."

"Eldon, Allen, Earl. It's all so confusing for a poor foreigner like myself." He sat down at the head of the table, his associate sitting next to him. This left an empty seat on each side of the table, one between Dexter and Negron, and one between the other man and myself.

"Your English is flawless, sir, let me assure you," Don laid it on thick, which seemed to be just the way Negron was used to being addressed, because he visibly preened at the praise.

He gestured to his left.

"This is my close associate, Alejandro Luis." The man nodded around the table.

Negron then seemed to notice me for the first time. He smiled broadly.

Diamond White

"And you, my dear. Forgive my manners in the confusion of so many introductions. Are you an Allen, or an Eldon, or perhaps an Alden?"

I matched his smile with my best.

"I'm a Wrigley."

"Like the—"

"—stadium."

"—chewing gum?"

"Or chewing gum," I said, amiably.

"And what is your position in this intriguing organization?"

If he says secretary I'm going to kill him. I won't even open the pencils, I'll just use them to poke out his eyes.

"I'm a lawyer."

"Oh, how delightful!"

"Really?"

He laughed. "No, not really, but you are very pretty, so I did not want to offend."

"*Señor* Negron, I must interrupt," said Dexter, by now disturbed by the knowledge that we had played him, and were now clearly up to something more than setting up a business deal.

Uncle Elgort spoke for the first time since sitting down.

"I think Mr. Dexter is anxious to give you your diamonds back," he suggested.

Dexter's face blanched, his droopy chin drooping further as his mouth fell open in panic.

"No, it's them, *señor*, they—"

"You have my diamonds for me, Jared?" asked Negron, holding out his hand.

"No! It's them, they can't be trusted!" His voice rose in pitch and volume. "They will betray you!"

Negron laughed. "Betray me? But we don't even have a partnership yet. They cannot possibly betray me. You,

Diamond White

however," he said, raising his right pointer finger in the air. Instantly one of the largest of the henchman was at his side. Negron pointed at Dexter and the big guy moved around behind the poor man, who's mouth was now flapping like a fish. "You and I *do* have a partnership, and that included you laundering my diamonds for me. Is it possible that you lost them at the laundromat?"

The large man leaned down slightly and snaked his big right arm around Dexter's neck, pulling back firmly. Dexter grabbed at the forearm with both hands, but he'd have had better luck lifting a telephone pole.

"Salerno," he hissed. "She took them, I swear."

Negron shook his head slowly. "Oh no, Jared. No, no, no. I have my own arrangement with Selena, so I know that you are lying. And now, now I know that you will lie and put another member of our team in harm's way to further your own purposes. I'm afraid our partnership is over."

He made a dismissive flicking motion with his hand, and Henchman Number One started to choke Dexter harder. We all sat up in alarm, but it was Elgort who spoke first.

"Please, Mr. Negron. We need to keep a low profile here in the Institute, especially today. Disposing of a body would not be easy, and would draw the sort of attention we don't need."

Negron seemed to consider for a moment, then nodded at the henchman, who released his grip. Dexter flopped forward, smacking his already bruised cheekbone on the hard table, unconscious but seemingly still alive.

I didn't really have much of a part in this negotiation, but now seemed like a good time to step in.

"*Gracias, Señor* Negron. It is very possible that we will need Mr. Dexter's services again in the future, as he has excellent contacts in the city government." I smiled. "I'm sure a man with your business reach understands the importance of that."

"But of course." He made another motion, and the henchman picked Dexter up under the arms and carried him away from the table, depositing his slumping body in one of the auditorium seats.

Don took this opportunity to get the conversation going again.

"Actually," he began, "I think it's only fair to tell you that Mr. Dexter was quite right about a couple of facts."

Both Negron and Alejandro Luis focused their attention on Don as he continued. "First, we do not currently have a partnership, and to be honest, we did not invite you to this meeting to offer you one."

"No?" Negron's dark eyebrows went up.

"No. We would like to offer you a straight-up sale agreement."

"Sale of what?" asked Luis. "What are you selling? Protection? We do not need protection."

"No," said Don, "you misunderstand. We are not selling, we are buying."

"You want to increase the number of guns?"

"No, we want to buy your business. Outright. We want you to stop operating in Chicago."

Luis snorted.

"That's ridiculous," Negron spat. "We came here for this nonsense?" At the edge of the space, the eight guards that Negron had brought to the meeting heard the change in his voice and suddenly became alert. From my viewpoint, I could see several of them reach for their empty holster, and see the frustration register on their faces. I looked to my right and saw Elgort's right hand slide down and into his pocket. Meanwhile, his left hand rested gently on the brass head of his cane.

Diamond White

"Please," said Don, holding up both hands in a calming gesture. "Please, sir. My research suggests that you are a keen business man, so please let me walk you through our proposal before you say no."

"Why should I listen to you? I don't even know who you are, and you try and scare me off. Pfft!"

Don nodded, staying smooth.

"A reasonable objection. First, let me say that we are wealthy, and it is in both our best interests if you move your operation to a different city, any city. We don't care, as long as it's not Chicago. You are making probably only fifty to sixty thousand dollars a month selling guns through Dexter to the bangers in the city."

Negron glanced at Luis, who nodded.

"There's a limit to that market, there's only so many guns that people can buy before you reach a saturation point. I know," Don said, holding up his hand to halt Luis's interjection. "I know, the plan is to buy back those guns and sell them again, over and over. But you can see how that very plan precludes the need for a fresh supply of guns. That's why we'd like to offer you four million dollars to cease operations anywhere in Chicago."

Luis snorted. "You forget sir, other opportunities. What Mr. Dexter referred to as ancillary avenues."

"You mean bringing in drugs, trafficking, et cetera?" asked Elgort.

"I'm sorry, that will be our purview as well," said Don flatly. "But we have something for you that will both assuage your financial loss and also be a small demonstration of our resourcefulness." He nodded at me.

I reached into my inside suit jacket pocket and pulled out the pouch of diamonds. Slid them down the table. They were the real ones. I couldn't take a chance on Negron or Luis being a diamond expert and blowing the whole scene on the spot, just to satisfy my attraction to those white, sparkly, beautiful diamonds.

Luis drew one out of the bag and held it up to the light, nodding.

"This is not so big a deal," he said, "stealing from Dexter. He is not very formidable." He handed the bag to Negron.

"Sure," I said, turning to look at him, "but have you met Selena Salerno? Cause she wanted those back badly."

Negron looked at me with a little twinkle in his eye. I couldn't tell if he wanted to kill me or kiss me. Maybe both.

"Surely," said Elgort in his stately voice. "There are other places where your business acumen could be put to use. Places where you do not have a small but potent contingent determined to make things difficult for you. It just makes sense. And, four million dollars plus the diamonds is a very fair price. It is our first and best offer."

"Your first and best offer?" Negron threw his hands up in the air. "Is that a threat?"

"Well," said Don, keeping an eye on the group of henchman, who seemed to have edged a bit closer, fanning out behind Negron's chair like sentinels. "it's not exactly a threat, it's just that it's better than our second or third offer."

"You make no sense," said Luis. "Why would your second offer be worse? Why wouldn't we just take what we want. You've shown no real ability to be a threat to us."

"Is that what you'd like," said Elgort, coldly and calmly. "A demonstration of our power?" There was a steely glint in his eye.

"*Sí*," said Luis. "We frankly are not so far impressed."

Don turned from him and addressed Negron.

"Antonio, your secretary seems a little put out."

Diamond White

Oooh, go Don. Switching to first name and insulting Luis all in one little sentence. The man belonged on the stage.

"But I'd like to remind you that not all power is physical power. Yes, you have some impressive henchmen, and I'm sure there are hundreds more like them back where you come from. But we come from here. Chicago. We draw our power from here, and will always have resources here unknown to you."

Don rolled on before they could interrupt. "Due to your skepticism, we now withdraw our first offer. Our second offer is simply that you go away and don't come back. You can keep the diamonds, but no cash. If you still insist that we prove ourselves to you, then we move on to our third offer."

Negron stood, and with him Luis.

"This has been all very entertaining, but like you say, this is not a good place for dead bodies, even if you had some way of making that happen. It's time for you to, as they say, put up or shut up."

"Very well," said Don, who also stood, moving behind Elgort's chair. He took his smart phone out of his breast pocket. "Our third and final offer is that you leave Chicago forever, and you pay us the 3.72 million pesos that you currently have in the bank of Mexico City."

At the sound of the precise number there was a startled look on Alejandro Luis's face. He looked at Don as Don pressed a button on his phone, which emitted a small beep.

"I'm sorry to keep you so long," said Don, putting the phone back in his pocket, and placing his hands on the back of Elgort's chair. "An associate of ours is very good with computers, but I made the mistake of directing him toward *your* smartphone, Tony, when actually," he gestured at Luis, "it turns out that it is your butler's phone that has access to all of the accounting and financials of Popocatépetl Incorporated. So, it took a little longer."

Luis had pulled his smartphone from his pocket, and stared at it in horror. I discreetly pushed my chair back from the table. It appeared that the meeting might be over.

Luis stabbed uselessly at the frozen screen and then threw the smartphone across the auditorium, where is smashed on the cement aisle.

"Too late," said Don.

"Kill them!" yelled Negron.

Don yanked Elgort's chair backward, onto the two back legs, and began to drag the old man backward to the door, which they were the closest to. Elgort held his cane in his left hand as he pulled the revolver from his right pocket.

All eight of Negron's men were rushing the man and his great nephew at once, the three furthest back pushing forward, unable to see the threat of the gun until the front five leapt out of the way.

Bang, bang, bang! The gun fired three times, the rubber bullets finding their mark. Two of the men went down hard, but the third, a huge guy with a crew cut took the bullet square in the chest and kept barreling toward them.

Elgort grimaced, and fired again, hitting the man in the groin and the thigh before he went down. In the moment the sightline was clear, Elgort fired the last shot straight at Negron, missing him but hitting Luis in the side of the neck. The rubber bullet broke the tender skin there and blood spurted out and spattered across the long table, which I just happened to be in the process of sliding under.

Diamond White

At this point Don was about five feet from the exit door, and the five remaining henchman were back in pursuit. He whistled loudly and half a second later the door to the room was pulled open by Jorge Alvarez, who had been waiting just outside.

As the chair slid out the door, Elgort tossed his brass tipped cane to Jorge who grabbed it out of the air and swung it into the knee of the first pursuer. He hit the second man in the face, and the third in the chest, but was unable to extract the cane from the man's grip. With a jerk, the man pulled Jorge to him and grabbed the front of his shirt.

I didn't see what happened next because Negron yelled, "Get the *puta!*" as I popped up on the opposite side of the table as him.

"Get me yourelf, jerkwad," I spat at him as I leapt on to the table and sent a kick at his head. He blocked, just, and I jumped off the table and on top of the arm he had used to shield the kick. I got purchase on his wrist as we both crashed to the floor, pulling his arm up between my legs and twisting it hard with both hands until I heard his elbow snap.

He screamed in pain, and suddenly I was off him and airborne. One of the henchman had run to his aid and simply grabbed me around the waist and thrown me across the room. I landed hard against the first row of auditorium chairs, right next to Jared Dexter, who was still unconscious. I managed to miss the arms of the chair and was cushioned, slightly, by the upholstery. It still winded me.

I sat up and looked around. There were only five people left in the room: Dexter, unconscious; Luis, unconscious and bleeding; Negron, curled on the floor yelling Spanish obscenities; myself; and the henchman, who was coming at me with an angry look on his face. I

195

Diamond White

had hurt Daddy, after all. The three henchman that had been shot with the rubber bullets had all staggered to their feet and out the door, hellbent on catching the old man that had wounded them. I had no idea what happened to Jorge, but he was gone, too. A rubber bullet hurts like hell, and can even kill you if it catches you in just the right place, but these guys were tough and now they were mad.

I scrambled backward up the aisle between seats. I glanced at Negron and saw him use his good arm to reach into his breast pocket and pull out his phone, presumably to call for reinforcements. I can't say that idea appealed to me.

As Henchy started up the aisle toward me I raced down one of the rows, then hopped over the chair back and over the next and the next until I was back at the front. There was no time to look back for my pursuer; I raced across the floor and threw myself on Negron, grabbing his hand around the wrist as he was trying to push a number into his phone. I sat heavily on his broken elbow, and he loosened his grip enough to allow me to wrench the phone free from his other hand. He may even have passed out, I didn't know because just as I grabbed the phone I was again picked completely off the ground and thrown across the room. This seemed to be Henchy's favorite move.

Fortunately, he threw me in the direction of the door. I landed on my feet, but the momentum was too much and I fell sprawling across the floor. The green and red pencils Nick had given me flew out of my pocket and rolled in front of me. I got to my knees as he grabbed me by the hair and the back of the jacket. He was intending to launch me into the air once again, but both my hair and my jacket came off, leaving me in a heap on the floor. The force of his own momentum made him

Diamond White

stumble back a few steps, a surprised look on his face as he stared at the black wig in his hand.

I didn't waste my chance. I grabbed the pencils, scrambled to my feet, and raced out the door and into a scene of utter chaos.

33

I'd been in the Modern Wing dozens of times to look at the art. I'd been there for two different weddings.

I'd never been there for a riot.

The riot ambiance was quite different. As I ran along the second-floor balcony, I was struck first by the noise. Shouts, occasional gunfire, screams of visitors caught in this unexpected nightmare.

It was clear what had happened. Security had responded, in force, to the sound of gunshots when Elgort fired the revolver. The responding officers and security guards had run straight into Negron's men as they raced after Don and Elgort, who were now nowhere in sight.

There were several dead or wounded officers on the ground. Negron's men had overpowered them and taken their weapons. I assumed they had called for reinforcements, and that the police had also called for reinforcements. Soon there would be dozens of armed men assaulting each other in the middle of the greatest art collection on the planet. What the hell had we done?

I glanced up toward the sculpture garden and the foot bridge. That was one way out. No sign of the Shelbys. This made me think of Nicky; I hoped he had left before any of this started. Marty, too, who had been stationed with his laptop in the gift shop downstairs, right below our meeting room.

I turned and headed down to the first floor instead, casting aside my glasses as I went down the stairs. Only Henchy had seen me without my wig, and now with my white blouse instead of my grey suit coat I was betting I could get out of here without any of Negron's other men noticing me. As long as I didn't get hit by a stray bullet, of course.

Diamond White

I made the first floor and began working my way toward the exit. Most of the museum guests were gone, out the door or hiding in the galleries or the gift shop. My guess was that Eldon and Elgort would blend in with them, and disappear through the exit. The henchmen were in a pitched battle with the police now, they wouldn't be able to keep track of who was where.

I made a run across the center of the hall, heading for the door. I was halfway across when I heard Negron's voice, shouting across the space.

"Stop!" he bellowed, and remarkably, for an instant, everyone did, even the cops. We all swiveled up to look at Negron on the cantilevered staircase, leaning heavily on Henchy, his left arm hanging at a horrible angle.

Negron scanned the crowd and then pointed straight at me.

"My diamonds!" he yelled.

Oops. Did I mention that I pocketed the pouch of diamonds when we were rolling around on the floor together? My bad.

"Kill her!" he shouted, and all eyes turned to me.

I was braced for the end as a shot rang out, followed suddenly by the shattering of the glass door to the street. Before the glass even hit the ground, a motorcycle raced through the opening, its engine roaring throughout the cavernous space.

While attention was diverted I dived behind the Cy Twombly sculpture in the middle of the room. People had broken from their trance, cops were yelling and men in dark suits were firing from positions staked out in the gift shop, the connecting windows all gone. A bullet ricocheted above my head.

I chanced a look around.

Negron was making his way, half carried, up to the third floor, likely looking to escape into the gardens over

Diamond White

the Nichols Bridgeway. The motorcycle had made it to the end of the gallery and turned around. The driver was dressed in a bright red, skin tight body suit. It could only be Selena Salerno.

She flipped up the face mask of her red helmet.

"I see you, Red Riley!" she shouted, and started back down the concourse toward me. How did she always recognize me? I had nowhere to go, so I straightened into a fighting stance, even though I had no chance against Salerno in a fist fight, never mind Salerno on a motorcycle.

But, up on the second floor galleries, two brave security guards rushed a bodyguard who was searching the gallery, most likely still looking for the Shelbys. They hit him hard, with momentum, and all three of them broke through the floor to ceiling glass, tumbling downward into Griffin Court, and right into the path of the motorcycle.

Salerno tried to swerve, but her front tire hit the leg of one of the guards, sending her skidding to the side. She separated from the motorcycle, coming to a halt on her back in the middle of the floor.

A police officer stepped forward, gun trained on her prone form, but he was almost immediately shot by one of Negron's men. I screamed as the shot echoed away and the officer dropped to the ground. A brief moment of silence followed; the cops in the building had lost. Two of Negron's men stood battered and bruised just outside the gift shop, holding pistols that had belonged to the police. One of them had shot the cop, then trained his gun on Salerno. The other had his gun pointed at me. I raised my hands up to shoulder height in surrender, my red pencil clutched in my fist.

Diamond White

In the near distance, the sound of police sirens could be heard through the shattered doors. Lots of sirens. And close.

One of the men looked up at Negron, who had made it to the third floor.

"Boss?" he said, indicating Selena on the floor, still unmoving.

"She's compromised," Negron growled in a low voice. "I have no more need of her. Kill them both and bring me the diamonds."

The man nodded and then brought his gun down and aimed it at Selena's chest, which was when I shot him in the face with the blow dart. He screamed and reeled backward, tripping over the motorcycle and falling to the ground clutching his face, his gun firing wildly off to the side.

The second man turned on me. Tires squealed as cop cars jumped the sidewalk, blocking the doors. As he pulled the trigger, Selena swept his feet out from underneath him, the bullet whizzing above my left shoulder.

He fell heavily on top of her, but she wasted no time headbutting him with her helmet and rolling him to the side.

I didn't stay to see the rest, I yanked the motorcycle upright and jumped on, leaving a long strip of black rubber across Renzo Piano's beautiful floor as I headed away from the police pouring in through the door and back deeper into the museum.

All the people were gone. I weaved in and out of the Asian art, careful not to hit anything. Of all the strange things that had happened this month, this was the strangest: cycling alone through the abandoned Institute.

My reverie was interrupted however by the approaching grand staircase. I bumped down it and into

Diamond White

the ticketing and information area. I killed the engine and jumped off the bike, letting it fall over on its side. I ran into the coatroom just as I heard police cars pulling up in front of the main entrance. I grabbed a random trench coat off the rack and headed for the door just as the first officers, decked out in full tactical gear, burst through.

I screamed in terror.

"Get down!" the first one yelled.

Instead I raised my hands in the air, the trench coat still gripped in my left hand.

"Don't kill me! I just needed my coat!"

A rough hand grabbed me around the waist and half-pushed, half-carried me to the door.

"You can't be in here ma'am, this is a terrorist attack!"

I screamed again as he pushed me out the door and down the steps past the lions and into the crowd of people gathered there. My head was aching, I may have broken a rib, and my heart was pounding wildly, but I couldn't help but smile to myself. I slipped into the trench coat and blended into the crowd, turning up the collar as I hurried off down the sidewalk.

A light rain was beginning to fall.

34

An hour later I was sitting at the big table on the fourth floor of Shelby Furniture. I was showered and dressed in jeans and a tank top from the clothing collection they kept there. I'd consumed four Advil and two Tylenol with Codeine. I had my hands wrapped around a hot mug of tea, and was having trouble keeping my eyes open.

"And then," Don says, more animated then I'd ever seen him, "just as the guy puts his hand on my shoulder, Ruby steps up behind him and throws a belt around his neck!"

"My belt!" offered Ellery Park, from her seat across the table.

"So Ellery catches Uncle Elgort, who's about to fall because I lost my balance. Ruby puts her foot into the back of the guys knee and brings him crashing down, his head hits the marble, and he's out."

I shook my head. "When did you get there?"

"We'd been there the whole time," Ruby explained, trying not to act too proud of herself. "We weren't sure what was going to happen, but when it did, whoo boy, it wasn't hard to miss."

She saw the pained look on my face.

"What is it?"

"The art."

"Well, we'll find out, I'm sure," said Nick, putting his hand on my shoulder, "but most of the shooting was in the great hall. There's not much there except glass."

"The Twombly got hit," I said.

"Yeah," replied Park, "but no one is ever going to be able to tell the difference."

Everyone laughed. There was no getting around it, Park was great kid. Smart, enthusiastic, skilled. I'd done my best to keep her at arm's length, I didn't really her

205

involved in all this, but here she was at the table. I'd failed completely; she was one of us.

"I'm so sorry I left!" Marty blurted suddenly. "I should have helped, but I didn't realize it was going to get all Reservoir Dogs."

"You did your part, brilliantly," Don assured him. "Nick found us, and we were able to get Uncle Elgort and all of us into the elevator just as the shooting started. We went down to the first floor and back into the main part of the museum, and by that time they were evacuating. We just walked out with everyone else."

I looked at Marty. "The bad guys set up shop in the shop, so if you hadn't left when you did you would have been in serious trouble."

Marty ran his hand through his hair, clearly still incredulous about the entire thing. "The gunfight, though, that wasn't part of the plan, was it?"

"No!" said Don and I at the exact same time.

"Well what happened?"

"Greed," said Elgort, from his end of the table. He looked very, very tired. "We made them a very good offer to walk away, and they wouldn't do it. Greed is not good," he said, and I could feel his eyes on me.

I took the pouch of diamonds from the pocket of my jeans and tossed it on the table.

"You never cease to intrigue me, Kay Riley," said Elgort, and everyone looked at me.

I raised my eyebrows.

"The rubber bullets."

Oh, that.

"I should be furious," Elgort continued, "but for some reason I'm not. Perhaps it's the humanity behind the gesture."

"I'm sorry, I just didn't want us to kill anyone."

"And yet many people are dead."

Diamond White

"Not by our hand."

"Does it make a difference?"

"Maybe." I met his gaze. "It would have made a difference to my dad, and I guess that's my barometer these days: What would Dad have done."

"He would have taken the diamonds?" asked Park in surprise.

"Oh yeah," I said, and laughed. "Hell yeah, he would have."

"Yes," agreed Elgort, smiling. "I believe you're right."

35

It was December at Ruby's place in Nippersink when Selena Salerno caught up with me. I had looked for some sign of her after the museum escapade, but she had once again slipped away. No record of arrest, no police warrants issued.

For several weeks I kept a motion sensor on in my living room, expecting each night to be the night she turned up, still looking for the diamonds. Who knows, despite saving her life, I had stolen her motorcycle and left her lying on the floor of the gallery. Maybe she held a grudge. Maybe Negron had taken her or killed her.

That's right, Negron escaped, too. Several of his men were arrested, but they all, to a man, spoke only Spanish and refused to respond to any of the cops' questions. Soon lawyers turned up and everything descended into a slow-boiling slog of bureaucracy. Not one of them, according to Ruby's inside information, would reveal who they worked for.

Jared Dexter was arrested, and will probably spend a few years in a very cushy high-end designer prison somewhere downstate, likely the same place they send all the former governors to. He, also, did not name Negron. The guy is Teflon.

I decided to take Ellery Park on my team, despite misgivings. Hopefully, I would be able to persuade her to go to law school, or something like that. Hell, maybe *I'd* go to law school. I can't run around vigilanteing forever. I just made that verb up.

Between September and Thanksgiving, Park and I worked together on several cases that Ruby unearthed. She had taken to studying police reports every night, looking for patterns. People or places that kept popping up, deserving a second look.

Diamond White

We also did a few small jobs for Uncle Elgort, but nothing near as grand or crazy as what we went through with Dexter.

Mostly, we hung out up at the lake and practiced. Getting stronger, getting smarter, learning new tricks. Nick would come up on the weekends and paint the lake, and I would sit next to him reading. History, novels, mysteries; I read whatever caught my eye at the library.

Winter came hard and early, with lots of snow. The day before Selena turned up, it had been a near white-out. When she tripped the camera alarm Marty had set up, I could barely see her on the monitor because she was dressed all in white. It was a miracle that we managed to subdue her. Despite all our practice, she was still an order of magnitude more proficient at fighting than we were. And it's possible that she wasn't trying too hard to hurt us. She wanted our help.

We helped her up out of the snow just as Ruby came flying out the back door with a shotgun in her hands, skidding to a stop at the top of the porch steps.

"Woah," I cried out. "It's okay. She's hurt."

Ruby kept her eyes, and the gun, on Salerno all the way up the steps and into the house, where we helped the woman into the kitchen and into a chair. Her white jumpsuit had red bloodstains all over it. It was disgusting, but Selena just sat there calmly, holding an icepack to her head while she told us why she was there.

Six months ago, not long after Selena had finished working for Aldo Frances, her older sister Valentina had been captured by Negron. Since then, Negron had been forcing her into one job after another, each more dangerous than the last, dangling the life of her sister in front of her until she complied. This explained the change in demeanor between the Salerno I met in the spring, and the one that came after me this fall.

Diamond White

Now, she'd come after me again, but not to hurt me or steal from me.

No, believe it or not, she had actually come to ask me to help her.

And, believe it or not, I decided I would.

The End.

Excerpt from Solid Gold

Windsor. It sounds so regal, as in Duke of Windsor, or Lord and Lady Windsor. As I looked out across the rooftops, I pictured castle spires and maybe Big Ben, or that big Ferris wheel they have now...

"Riley!"

"Huh?" I snapped out of it and turned back to Selena, who was kneeling a few feet away, working on unlocking a small window on the upper floor of a warehouse in Windsor, Canada. We were standing on a lower roof, the little windows in front of us ran the length of the building to let natural light into the large open warehouse space.

"I said I've got it," she hissed.

"Sorry," I whispered back. "I was distracted by the horrible view. I expected Canada to be a lot more, I don't know, majestic." I could see my breath as I spoke, and I was grateful for the hour I had spent on the Athleta website buying cold-weather workout gear. The tights I bought were very warm, and I had a short jacket that was quilted and fitted, but still gave great range of motion to my arms. My red hair was finally long enough to get in my way, just, so I kept it tucked away under a black knit watch cap.

Selena stood up, sliding her small metal tools into a little pocket on the upper arm of her leather jacket. Under her jacket she was wearing her standard issue white Lycra jumpsuit, with a pair of knee-high black boots. Her legs must have been freezing, but she would never show it. She leaned close to me so she could speak quietly.

"I cannot see the women. But there are signs of habitation—table and chairs, little kitchen area—but no surveillance cameras that I can see. Also," she added, "I count seven guards, and there is at least one out front."

Diamond White

"Eight?"

"That I can see."

"How do you feel about that number?"

"It's a little high," she admitted.

"A little?"

"Shh. Keep your voice down. Just follow my lead."

She took her jacket off and dropped it, then turned back to the window. It hinged at the top, and she pushed quietly on it until it opened inward. Her feet slid through and then her hips and then her head and she was gone. I squatted down and peered through the window. Selena had picked a good spot. The entire upper floor was just a balcony, about ten feet wide, all the way around the outside of the warehouse. You could have held track practice on it, it was probably a quarter mile if you followed it all the way around and back again. Large crates were stacked in the area just below the window, and I could see Selena crouched behind them, already sneaking looks over the railing to the floor below. From my vantage point I could only see one guard, dressed in black pants and a tight black t-shirt that showed his impressive—to him—muscles. He had a shoulder holster, and was holding something small in one hand that I couldn't make out. He brought his hand up to his mouth, and took a big bite. It was a sandwich. Clearly these guys were on low alert status. Well, they'd be sorry for that.

I took off my coat. Underneath I had a shoulder holster of my own, and I made sure the security strap was properly snapped. Nothing more embarrassing than having your firearm clatter to the floor when you're performing some amazing gymnastic feat. I kept my gloves on. They were light and flexible, and I wore them not just for the cold, but to disguise the fact that I was missing two fingers from my left hand.

Diamond White

I waited until sandwich man turned to grab his water bottle from the table behind him, and slid through the window. It was a short drop to the balcony deck, and in seconds I was squatting down next to Selena. She turned to me and winked, then pointed to the far end of the balcony, where another guard was just entering through a door that most likely led to a staircase. He looked left and right and then started ambling slowly clockwise around the perimeter of the balcony. Selena and I shifted to the far side of the largest crate to be sure he would not see us until it was too late.

I was tapping my fingers on my thigh, for some reason the song "Beautiful Day" by U2 was running through my head. I don't think I'd heard that song in ages. In fact, my clearest memory of it was my high school friend Alex playing it in her car, constantly, our senior year. She used to drive me everywhere. My Dad didn't think I should have unrestricted use of a car, even though we had one just sitting in the garage, since Mom didn't drive anymore.

I looked over at Selena. I wondered what her high school was like, on Isla Grande, way down off the coast of Chile. I'm sure the music was different. Did her older sister, Valentina, drive her to school? What kind of cars did they have there. Did they have cars?

Selena noticed me staring at her in a strange way, and made a face back. Then she put one hand over my tapping fingers and held the other to her lips. We could hear footsteps approaching our location. We both readied in our crouch. Ideally we would let him walk by and take him from behind, but it was likely he would see us when he got level with our location.

Selena let go of my hand and pointed at herself, then pointed up in the air, then she pointed at me and then pointed down to the ground. While I was pondering what

Diamond White

this meant, she held up four fingers and then folded them down one at a time in a countdown. Four, three, two, one.

On one, she uncoiled like a striking snake, leaping six feet in the air just as the man came around the corner of the crates. She wrapped her left arm around his head, catching his mouth in the crook of her elbow, and swung around on to his back, wrapping her legs around his torso.

Less elegantly, I rolled forward and wrapped both my arms around his legs, just below the knee. He flailed one arm back, over his head to try to grab Selena, while his other hand reached for the pistol in his shoulder holster. Selena leaned back out of his grasp, which had the added benefit of pulling him backward. With his legs immobilized he began to fall, at which point Selena unwrapped her legs and planted them easily on the ground, catching his weight without releasing her left arm from around his face. Her right arm beat him to his holster and pulled his pistol up and high into the air, smashing it into his temple as the two of them sunk slowly to the floor, his immense weight slowly buckling Selena's knees until she lay on her back on the wood floor with the unconscious man on top of her.

The entire exchange had barely caused a sound, the loudest noise being that of the impact of the gun butt on the guard's skull. I released his legs and sat up. About all I could see of Selena was her left arm sticking out from underneath the man, flopping frantically. Still kneeling, I got both hands under his left hip and heaved until he rolled off her and came to rest face down next to her.

Selena gasped as the weight was taken off her chest, and pulled her right arm out from under the guard, his gun still clenched in her right hand. She looked at me and I gave her the thumbs up and winked. She sat up and rolled her eyes. Her white, skin tight body suit now had dirt all over it. Why she didn't wear black I just don't know. She laid the gun on the man's back and used both hands to straighten and tighten her pony tail, then picked the gun back up and removed the magazine. She checked the chamber to make sure it was empty, then she stood up and looked around. I pointed to the largest stack of crates and she nodded, then stepped on the guard's back to give her enough height to put the magazine out of sight on top of the highest crate.

At her signal, we rolled the guard on to his back, and Selena laid two fingers against the side of his neck to see if he was still alive, though I could tell by the rise of his chest that he was. She gripped his neck with both hands, then looked over at me. I shook my head. I watched her eyes as her brain worked for a moment, then she nodded slightly and removed her hands. Selena didn't like killing people any more than I did, but I also knew that she wanted severe punishment for anyone involved in the kidnapping of her sister. When we went downstairs, I knew that decisions would be made faster, and with less regard for the victims. But, for now, we seemed to be in agreement.

I pointed to his big black boots. I took the left and she took the right and we removed the long black laces, rolling him back on his stomach to tie his hands and feet. I wasn't worried about a gag, the other guards would know we were here long before this guy woke up.

Selena finished tying his hands behind his back. Then, as if in afterthought, she grabbed his pinky finger and bent it back until we both heard it snap. Ugh, it made my stomach do a flip. She grabbed his third finger but I put my hand on her shoulder to stop her. She looked up at me and grimaced, but let go of his hand and stood up.

Diamond White

We looked to our left and to our right, but there was no one else on the balcony. She pointed to the door that the guard had come out of, and then pointed at me. I pointed back at her and raised my eyebrow in the universal eyebrow sign for "What will you be doing?"

Selena tilted her head toward the other end of the warehouse, and made a looping motion with her index finger. Whatever the hell that meant.

We parted ways, both clinging to the shadowy brick wall of the warehouse. From this position, I couldn't see down to the first level, but that meant that they couldn't see me either. As I moved quietly toward the far end, I passed other stacks of crates, a pallet filled with cardboard boxes with Samsung printed on the outside, the whole pallet wrapped in clear plastic, and assorted other cargo. It seemed there was more being trafficked through here than women. Negron's empire was ever-expanding.

I reached the far wall of the warehouse. Straight in front of me was a big metal loading door. I guess that's how they get cargo up here. I kept it in mind as a potential escape route, should that become necessary.

I rounded the corner and cautiously approached the open doorway, my ears straining for the sound of footsteps. I could hear men talking indistinctly on the lower level, but the sound seemed to come from the other end of the warehouse.

I moved through the door and into a dark stairwell. I steadied myself with one hand against the wall while I quietly removed my boots and set them next to each other in the corner. I took my socks off for good measure; slipping on the floor and wiping out would be unprofessional, and I wanted to be professional. Selena seemed to consider me an amateur who was well meaning, and occasionally lucky, but that's about all the credit she gave me. Except, of course, that she had asked me to help her. Why me? Didn't she have anyone else in her life she could rely on? I said a silent thank you to Nick and Don and Marty and Ruby and El.

As I rounded the landing and started down the last few steps, I could see out the doorway and into the large warehouse. Along the right hand side, where I had come from, the lower level contained more boxes, as well as shelves filled with dry goods, canned food, and towels and clothing folded and stacked. On the left side, the lower level wall was flush with the edge of the balcony, there was no overhang. Instead, doors were set into the wall every ten feet or so. Some of them looked like regular office doors, but three of them had serious locks on the outside and small square windows set at head height. These ones looked like prison cells, and they probably were.

From where I stood, in the shadows of the stairwell, I had to squint to see the far end of the warehouse, but I could make out a kitchenette, a hallway that probably led to the front door, and four guys sitting around a table playing cards. There was a guy standing at the entrance to the hallway, half alert while smoking a cigarette. An automatic rifle was leaning up against the wall nearby. This was apparently the guy on active duty.

In the kitchenette, a tall man with a bald head was standing at the stove, sautéing something—I was too far away to get a whiff, but I could hear the crackle of the food in the frying pan over the sound of the men arguing about the card game.

Suddenly, my eye caught movement up above, a quick flash of white as Selena moved in to position, crouched next to a fork lift. I moved forward slowly, closer to the light, until I was sure she could see me through the doorway. She nodded at me, then subtly made a pointing

Diamond White

signal, indicating her right, my left. I leaned closer to the doorway, slowly edging forward until I could see around the door jamb, then pulled my head quickly back. Leaning against the wall, about eight feet from the doorway, was another lackadaisical guard, his gun in his hands but slack. He was watching the guys at the other end of the warehouse, wishing he were in the game, and never turned his head toward me or looked up to where Selena was hidden.

I caught her eye again from my place in the shadows. I drew my weapon from my holster and showed it to her, then pointed in the direction of the guard. She nodded. I moved my gun to my left hand and with my right I held up four fingers, then pointed toward the card table (I only had three fingers on my left hand). Then I held up one finger and pointed toward the front door, and then I held up one finger again and pointed toward the kitchen. Selena nodded each time, then made that weird rolling motion with her index finger in front of her. I had no idea what she meant, and gave an exaggerated shrug. We really should get those tiny earphones that fit right inside your ear. How 'bout it, Technology Acquired? I'd ask Marty when we got back.

Selena got up from her crouch into a standing position, still in the shadow of the fork lift. She held up her left hand and closed one finger at a time, counting down four three two one.

With two quick bounds she leaped into the air, bracing her hands on the railing and then going up and over, somersaulting twice before landing in a crouch on the card table, which promptly collapsed under the sudden and extreme force.

As you can imagine, bedlam ensued. Two of the men had their thighs and knees crushed by the collapsing table and hollered in pain, the other two jumped back as

Diamond White

Selena leapt between them, hit the ground in a crouch and then sprang forward into a flying side kick that caught the door guard in the chest just as he was reaching for his rifle.

Down at my end of the warehouse, the guard sprang off the wall and began to run toward the ruckus. He made it ten feet before I fired my X2 Taser gun into his back, running up behind him as he turned back toward me, stumbling. He raised his weapon and fired at me but his aim was already impaired, and before I even reached him he had fallen to his knees, one hand reaching over his shoulder to try and pull out the prongs.

Without stopping, I sprinted past, sending him sprawling with a kick as I went by. I released the cartridge from the end of the taser, and broke into a full sprint up the length of the open space, my bare feet hardly making a sound.

I was closing the distance fast, but I was still thirty feet away when the man in the kitchen saw me. He shouted and pointed, but no one was listening to him. Of the two men who had been wounded by the crashing table, one was still curled on the ground, but the other had staggered to his feet and made his way to a CB radio that was on one of the shelving units. The two other card players had their backs to me as they fought with Selena. The man she had kicked in the chest seemed to be down for the count. I don't know if they thought two against one was going to be easy, or if they didn't think a girl could fight, but neither of them drew their pistol before approaching her. They'd pay for that.

As I closed the gap to fifteen feet, the man on the floor rolled over so he could see me, and without trying to get up he drew his pistol from his shoulder holster. I shot him with the taser and careened suddenly to the right, toward the cook, dropping the now-empty taser as

Diamond White

I went. It only held two cartridges. Something buzzed past my ear and then I heard the loud rapport of a pistol, but there was no point in looking back. Either the tasing would bring him down, or he'd shoot me in the back. We'd find out in a second.

Meanwhile, in front of me didn't look that great either. The cook, it seemed, was not just the cook but also one of the guards. Either that or he was a cook who just felt more comfortable with an AR15 by his side. He picked it up and aimed it at me. I was ten feet away, dead center in front of him. I ducked and tried to roll out of the way. Who was I kidding? I was a dead woman. For real this time.

Nothing happened. I came up out of the roll and onto my feet to see him fiddling frantically with the mechanical safety. Maybe he was just a cook after all. I grabbed a broom that was leaning against the wall, just as the cook brought the gun back up to fire. I stepped in, my hands spaced widely along the shaft of the broom, and blocked the barrel of the rifle out and to the side. The gun fired once, into the wall, and I dropped the broom and grabbed the barrel with both hands, kneeing the cook in the groin at the same time.

I could hear Selena fighting in the hallway, and then I heard a blast of static as the other man shouted into the CB in English: *We are under attack!*

Without letting go of the rifle I turned my body away from the cook and kicked down hard on his foot, forgetting I didn't have any shoes on. Son of a bitch, that hurt. There was another burst of static, then a voice over the CB responded: *You were told to never use this channel.*

I took my right hand off the rifle just long enough to elbow him in the face, and when I felt his grip loosen I yanked the rifle out of his hands, aimed it at the CB

221

radio, and fired three quick shots. The man using the CB dove to the ground, and at least one of the shots must have hit because the hissing static fell abruptly silent.

Secure the scene, Riley, I thought to myself, and swept the gun around the room. I could see the CB operator; I couldn't see around the corner and down the hall to where Selena was, but the two men I had hit with the taser were both down. I heard a sound behind me and turned to check on the cook, a moment too late. He brought the frying pan down hard, with both hands, onto the AR right near my hands, knocking it from my grasp and onto the floor. Good thing he went for the gun, if he'd hit my head like that it would have caved in like a pumpkin.

His forward momentum carried him past me. He swung wildly back around with the pan, hoping to catch me off guard, but I ducked under it, squatting all the way to the floor and coming back up with the broom again. He came at me again with the pan, but I blocked it with the broom handle. And again, and again. Christ, I thought, Selena knew what she was doing with the quarterstaff training.

I blocked his fourth swing, but his strength and the weight of the pan broke the broomstick in half, the end with the bristles flying out of my weak hand and landing on the open gas burner, the straw catching fire. The cook was a big man, with a bald head and a crooked nose. There were food stains on his t-shirt where he had wiped his hands while he was cooking. He had a grin on his face when he saw the broken broom, but it changed to a look of renewed concern when I thrusted at him with the pointed end. He tried to block with the pan, but it was too heavy, and I punctured his left shoulder with the tip of the broken handle. He grunted in pain, but otherwise kept coming at me.

Diamond White

Suddenly there was an explosion of brick just to our right, fragments hitting us both, stinging. Another gunshot and the wooden cabinet door above the stove splintered. The cook and I both turned to look across the room to where the CB operator was now standing with a pistol, firing at me, I suppose, but his aim wasn't that great.

Obviously, the cook felt the same way because he turned and shouted, "*Alto!*"

In the half-second this afforded me, I used my gloved hand to grab the other half of the broom from the hot stovetop and swing the burning end into the side of his head. He screamed and brought both hands to his face, dropping the frying pan. I let go of the burning broom and used a two handed grip to thrust the other half of the handle into his stomach. As he grunted and grabbed at the broom, another gunshot rang out, and he surged forward as it hit him in the back. He toppled down on top of me and we went over in a heap. His body protecting mine as three more shots were fired.

There was sudden silence. Hesitantly, I peeked up and over the cook's body. In the exact place where the CB operator had been standing, Selena Salerno now stood, holding the man's pistol. He was unconscious on the ground. She was sweating and breathing heavily, but was as alert as a jaguar.

"Is he dead?" she asked, motioning to the cook. I looked at his face, and his staring eyes told me all I need to know. I gulped and nodded, leaping to my feet and backing away from him, staring.

"Riley!" Selena hissed at me, breaking the moment.

"Right, right," I mumbled, and reached over and turned off the stove burner. The enflamed broom bristles had died out, and the AR-15 was lying on the floor in a puddle of the cook's blood. I turned away and took a deep breath.

"Do not throw up, Riley," Selena said in a severe voice. "It leaves too much DNA."

"Nice."

I moved away from the body and over to Selena, who was collecting a pistol and a set of keys from the body of the second man I had tasered. I looked back at Selena, who was still breathing heavily and leaning a bit to the left, one hand on her ribs.

"Are you okay?"

"It's nothing." She started across the open warehouse toward the wall with the locked doors.

"One of them called for back-up, Selena, we've got to hurry."

"Then help me," she said, and broke into a limping run.

Also By

The Red Riley Adventures:
Chicago Blue
Diamond White
Solid Gold
Agent Orange

The Levelers:
The Grafton Heist
The Train Job

Available wherever ebooks are sold, or at
andrewsauthor.com

Diamond White

Made in the USA
Middletown, DE
12 September 2023

38380821R00137